D0945032

EMPIRE
OF
LIGHT

EMPIRE
OF
LIGHT

DAVID CZUCHLEWSKI

G. P. PUTNAM'S SONS • NEW YORK

This is a work of fiction. Names, characters, places, and incidents either
are the product of the author's imagination or are used fictitiously,
and any resemblance to actual persons, living or dead, business
establishments, events, or locales is entirely coincidental.

G. P. Putnam's Sons
Publishers Since 1838
a member of
Penguin Group (USA) Inc.
375 Hudson Street
New York, NY 10014

Library of Congress Cataloging-in-Publication Data

Czuchlewski, David.
Empire of light / David Czuchlewski.
p.   cm.
ISBN 0-399-15103-6
1. Missing persons—Fiction.   2. Cults—Fiction.   I. Title.
PS3553.Z83E47   2003   2003041408
813'.6—dc21

Printed in the United States of America
1   3   5   7   9   10   8   6   4   2

This book is printed on acid-free paper. ∞

Book design by Chris Welch

TO KRISTINA

I had set my heart on shadows . . .

—AUGUSTINE, *Confessions*

PART ONE

ONE

WHEN I RECEIVED word that Anna Damiani Barrett was officially lost—lost, that is, for the first time—I was home for dinner with my parents. It was toward the end of the meal, my father already pushed back slightly from the table so that his large, tired body could unfurl in a slouch, my mother stacking plates and prodding the remains of the roast with the serving fork.

I drained the last of my beer and watched my father reach for his yellow legal pad. He ran his hand through his thick gray hair and considered the pad, on which he recorded, in the order of their occurring to him, matters that he needed to discuss with us. This was the phase of dinner in which plans were made, consensus reached. Anna had often remarked on the military atmosphere of the proceedings.

"He might as well have unfolded a map of Normandy on the table," Anna said to me once. "Your father is still the perfect soldier."

In many ways, she was right. My father maintained a humorless intolerance for disobedience. Even a trip to the local mall was an operation requiring precise planning and a rendezvous time. When I was young I found an old snapshot of him, in uniform, smiling in front of a dusty truck. I stashed the picture in my bureau drawer and occasionally took it out to wonder at, imagining that earlier, secret life.

Glancing up in my direction from his legal pad, he said, "Number one. There's a letter for you."

I was always retrieving mail when I came home, mostly credit card applications and statements about the accumulating interest on my student loans. Usually my father tossed the relevant envelope to me and moved on to another item on the list, but this time he exchanged a look with my mother and remained silent.

"The return address says *Barrett*," he said.

"Is it from Anna?"

"I don't read your mail."

He handed the letter to me with uncharacteristic gentleness. The envelope was cream colored, with a Central Park West return address that I remembered well. The paper was as thick and soft as vellum. The stationery inside bore a calligraphic insignia, CHB, in elegant black embossing. Once I saw that it was from Anna's stepfather, I was sure it would say that Anna was dead. With my eyes racing across the sentences, trying to absorb their meanings even before the individual words had registered, I read Carl Barrett's haphazard script:

Dear Matthew,

I hope this note finds you well. It has been too long since we have been in touch, and I regret that the occasion for my note is an unpleasant one. I am writing on behalf of Anna. It has been several months since I have heard from her. I am desperate to have some news of her, but all of my inquiries have been ineffectual. In case Anna contacts you or in case you hear some news about her, won't you please let me know?

Warm regards,

Carl Barrett

My parents were too polite to ask what it said, but I knew they were wondering.

"It's from her stepfather. He doesn't know where she is. He wants to know if I have any information."

"Do you?" my mother said.

"Of course not."

"The poor girl," my father said, shaking his head.

"What do you mean?" I said.

"It's not her fault, is it? I strongly believe that sometimes people can't help themselves."

"Oh right, I forgot. It's all just a quirk of brain chemistry, not a personal failing, right?"

"I just thank God that *you've* never given us problems like that," my mother said.

I felt a strong desire not to delve further into the topic of Anna's culpability or to open a philosophical discussion about the nature of addiction.

"I've got to get home," I said.

On the bus back to my apartment, I took out the letter and read it once more. So Anna was out there in some dim, sweaty room, probably drunk or high, wasting herself. I had made a point of not staying in touch after she dropped out of Princeton, and I'd had no idea where life had taken her. She could have gone through rehab, could have been living happily ever after in a distant state. But the letter proved that what I had suspected was true, and I realized I had known it all along.

The bus heaved and lurched through the dark, indistinguishable streets. I was the only passenger. Outside, the frame houses of Queens passed by, the empty churches, the brick bungalows, the muddy softball fields of my youth, all hidden in the night. When I reached my tiny apartment I tried to grade some papers, but I found I couldn't concentrate. When I tried to go to sleep I found I couldn't do that either, so I turned on the television and flipped around the channels. At some point, a dream incorporated the words from the set and I fell asleep.

THE NEXT DAY I put the letter from Carl Barrett in my desk drawer, beneath a hole puncher and a package of manila mailing envelopes, and I resolved to forget about it. I reasoned that it held no relevance to me, since Anna was simply a figure from the past. My memories of her were becoming by degrees less vivid and intrusive— although when I passed a group of feral, drugged-out runaways near the Port Authority that afternoon, I experienced a moment of panic, imagining Anna among them.

Late that night, there was a sharp and unexpected knock at my door. I did not stand on ceremony, and almost anyone I knew in New York would have been comfortable stopping by late and unannounced, but my friends didn't often wander past Sunnyside after midnight. Also, it was raining, the kind of steady and dispiriting storm that showed no signs of ending.

I opened the door and found Anna standing on the stoop in the cold rain, absolutely soaked. For a fraction of a second I questioned whether it was actually Anna. Her hair, which was wet and plastered to her head, was unexpectedly blond, supplanting the dark brown I had known and cherished. She was holding a copy of the *International Herald-Tribune* over her head to protect herself from the rain, but the paper had become ineffectual as an umbrella, soggy and warped.

Neither of us spoke, and the only sounds were the hissing of rain against concrete and the gurgling complaint of the drainpipe.

"Jesus," I said. It was a bizarre coincidence that she would arrive just after a note from Carl Barrett regarding her—a glimpse, perhaps, of some greater universal scheme that I could not as yet comprehend.

"Can I come in?"

"I'm sorry. I'm just so surprised."

I considered telling her she wasn't welcome, but doing so would have required a cold mastery of complex emotions and a denial of curiosity that I could not manage. I went to the bathroom and returned with a purple bath towel. She plunged her face into the soft terry and bent over, allowing her long hair to dangle. In that position she wrapped the towel around her hair, creating a purple turban.

Without a word she took a seat at my desk. I remained standing near the door, crossing my arms. She swiveled and tilted the chair, examining with casual interest the papers and pictures on my bulletin board.

"I don't want to put you out," she said. "But I was thinking it might be okay if I stayed here for a day or two."

Anna picked up the stapler from the desk and began absently un-hinging and reclosing the top. She glanced up with hopeful dark eyes. She was beautiful, but also so drawn and bedraggled that I doubted someone meeting her for the first time would acknowledge her beauty. It seemed that she had grown tired of keeping up appearances, that she had taken on a disguise to render herself more ordinary.

She removed a pack of cigarettes from her pocket and gestured with them, asking if she could. I shook my head to say no.

"Are you drunk?" I said.

"No," she said, sounding wounded by the implication.

"Why are you here?"

"I don't know. I just flew in from Italy. I was on the plane coming in to JFK and we were circling over the city. We were just a few hundred feet off the ground. We went around and around. The city was endless, just lights and highways and rain as far as you could see. I don't know why, but I thought of you being somewhere down there."

"You were in Italy to see your father?"

"Not really. I was just bumming around, having a good time."

"Does your stepfather know you're back?"

"Nope. I'm done with him for good now."

She unwrapped the towel from her head, letting her hair fall in wet, ropy curls. She draped the towel around her neck like a prizefighter.

"He just wrote me a letter," I said. "He wanted to know where you were."

She laughed bitterly, from a deep reserve of contempt. "Oh, I'm very impressed. There's dedicated parenting for you. Did he write in the letter that he had fucking disowned me?"

"What do you mean?"

"I mean he said, 'You are no longer my daughter,' and 'You're on your own now. From now on no money, no support, no nothing.'"

"I don't think you should stay here."

"I guess I'll have to borrow an umbrella, then."

She leaned backward in the chair, drying her hair with the towel, cocking her head to one side and working the area around the ear. Her damp shirt clung to the curves of her chest and shoulder and arm, and I felt a desire that was intense and illogical.

"Can't we be reasonable?" she said.

I didn't have the heart to throw her out. Nor did I foresee the extremes of confusion and distress to which, given a chance, she would lead me. I thought, what could be the harm in letting her crash for the night? It *was* raining pretty hard out.

"Fine. Stay for the night. But that's it. Just one night."

"God, I could use a drink. Have you got anything?"

SHOWERED, WEARING SOME spare shorts and a Princeton T-shirt that was too big for her, reclining on my mattress and waving her bare feet, Anna looked comfortable and relaxed, though tired. Next to her, on the floor, was a mug she was using as an ashtray. She had said she was going outside to smoke, but I relented and told her not to bother. The last time I had smoked was with her. I remembered the dry, sweet taste, the transcendent light-headedness of a deep inhalation, the antsy, low-grade need for another and another. I had quit as soon as we broke up, the difficulty of the chemical withdrawal hardly noticeable within another, more pervasive withdrawal.

I watched her drawing the smoke into her lungs, holding it in and releasing her ghostly breath, ritualistically tapping the cigarette against the mug. I resisted the impulse to ask for one. I was too strong to be defeated now, after so long without even feeling the craving.

In another mug was some sake from a bottle that had been knocking around the kitchen since the beginning of the year. It was a gift to me from a Japanese friend, but it tasted of paint thinner and I wouldn't drink it. I had stood in the kitchen considering the sake bottle, knowing that Anna would be delighted with it. The last thing she needed was someone to help her drink. It was a perverse decision to bring it to her, a form of surreptitious punishment. She didn't see it as such, and was drinking the stuff like milk.

The rain drummed softly and hypnotically on the window behind the bed. The only illumination was from my small desk lamp, which cast looming shadows on the walls. The room was warm and cozy, and I could almost forgive Anna for making herself so comfortable despite my studied silence.

"I'm going into the other room to do some work," I said, standing and gathering my papers. "I leave at seven tomorrow morning. You can let yourself out whenever you get around to it."

She nodded and looked down. "I understand. You don't even want to talk to me."

"I'm not falling for this shit. I said you could stay, but that's it. I don't want to have a big heart-to-heart with you. It's not healthy. We shouldn't have anything to do with each other."

"Don't you know why I'm here?"

"You had some sort of psychotic episode as your plane was landing."

"I'm here because I realized I made a mistake."

She folded her legs underneath her body and flopped sideways on the mattress, supporting her head with her arm. She was quiet, smoking silently. Just as I was about to give up and go grade my papers, she spoke in a low, halting monotone.

"I've lost track of something, and the last time I was on track was when we were together. On the plane I was thinking about what had gone wrong, where I had made the first step in the wrong direction. It all began when you and I broke up. When we were together was the last time everything was okay. And I just really wanted to see you again."

"And what did you think was going to happen? That we would get back together?"

"No, of course not . . . I don't know." She sighed. "I don't know what I want."

She rolled on the bed to reach the makeshift ashtray, stretching her arm to its full extension and revealing, underneath the baggy T-shirt, the feline curve of her shoulder blade. I wondered whether she knew the effect that her movements were having on me. I nearly decided that it would be worth the complications that would arise if only I could be with her again, even just for that one night. But then she took another slug of the sake and I remembered the sound of her vomiting in the men's-room toilet down the hallway from my dorm room, filling the bathroom stall with the sweet smell of barely digested tequila. I remembered having to soak masses of paper towels to clean her pink-flecked face and the sodden hair that had fallen in the way. I remembered her moaning, her face against the piss-stained tile floor, saying, incorrectly as it always turned out, "I'm okay. This won't happen again." She had made me miserable, and I wasn't going to fall for this new variation of her contrition.

"Enjoying the sake?" I said.

She nodded.

"Nothing's changed," I said.

She closed her eyes and turned away. I gathered my papers and my gradebook. She stubbed out the remainder of her cigarette in the bottom of the mug and threw herself backward into the pillow, arms crossed above her head.

"You're a sweetheart for letting me stay. I'll keep out of your way now."

I SLEPT ON the living-room couch, which in its advanced age had lost the ability to sufficiently cushion its crosswise metal beams. I woke like an old man, hand on the coccyx, wincing. Some impulse moved me to check on Anna before I left. The room retained the stale remainder of the previous evening's smoke. Anna was buried in the covers, sleeping on her side, her right arm thrown above her head as in a dance move. Her lips were parted, and each breath stirred a stray strand of hair that had fallen across her face. She looked young and untroubled. As I watched, the tickling of the hair on her face registered in her neglectful mind, and she ascended toward consciousness far enough to brush away the offending hair and murmur dreamily.

I taught poorly that day. I didn't have the papers graded, as I had promised. I was tired and my back remained sore for most of the morning. The kids had only two weeks of school left before summer vacation, and they were therefore even more difficult to control than usual. I was in no mood to walk around the room to keep them from talking to one another. I stared at my lesson plan on the voyages of the explorers. I looked up at the kids, with their glum and hostile expressions, and felt totally unequal to the task of making the peregrinations of Cortés relevant to them. It was not a banner day for Teach for Humanity.

On my way home I stopped for food at the corner grocery near my apartment. As I wandered the aisles I decided to prepare the one relatively elaborate dish I knew how to make, one that Anna had taught me to make in Sicily several summers before. I collected fettuccine, pine nuts, raisins, chard, garlic and Parmesan cheese. I evaluated the lettuce and picked a head of floppy red leaf, getting enough for two, on the off chance.

But the apartment was empty and silent, filled with the dim light of sunset and evening gloom. Anna had made the bed and washed the mugs she had used the previous night. There was a note, folded and slipped into the keyboard of my computer so that it stood upright.

> Dear Matt,
>
> Thanks again for letting me barge in last night. I got in touch with a friend who lives in Red Hook and she said I could stay with her for a while, so don't worry. It was good to see you again, although I guess also kind of awkward. I did a lot of thinking last night. I'm beginning to see that I'm the one responsible. I made a wrong turn and never realized it. I feel that everything is broken somehow. But I'm going to get my act together. Here I am in New York again, and there's no reason I can't start over. I want you to <u>want</u> to see me.
>
> Your friend,
> Anna
>
> P.S. Please don't tell Carl where I am.

I crumpled the note and pitched it across the room into the wastebasket. I hated the way she made me feel—sick with aloneness and infected with her craziness. That entire night I'd had to restrain myself from bursting into the bedroom to be with her. I knew she would not have refused.

I made dinner, enough for two, and ate alone. I turned on the evening news but I didn't pay attention to it. I almost picked up the phone to let Carl Barrett know I had seen Anna, but I decided I owed him nothing, not even that small favor. Sitting in my messy apartment, awash in the television's purple light, I knew for sure that something was missing—certainly Anna, but also something larger that her presence and renewed absence had simply alerted me to.

When I went to bed the pillow smelled faintly of her hair and the sake.

TWO

Dear Matt,

I just wanted to drop you a quick e-mail to let you know that every-thing is going absolutely great. I can't remember the last time I felt so optimistic. Priorities are key. To quote the great Giuseppe Conti, "There is no peace but through reflection and self-discipline."

I also want to say how truly sorry I am for messing everything up. I don't want to make excuses. I've accepted the fact that I have to live with the consequences of my actions. But I also want you to know that things really are different now. I'm attending counseling. I have been clean and sober since the day I left your apartment. It hasn't been easy. In the beginning I thought about drinking maybe once every minute. I'm down to a few times an hour. I got up this morning and went for a walk around Greenwich Village, and for the first time in months I was in a great mood. People around me were happy and the world was colorful and beautiful and worthwhile. I feel like I've been let out of a dark room, and my senses are coming alive again.

Here's the big news: the counseling is run by Imperium Luminis. Remember them?

My computer time is up. I'll tell more later.

Love,

Anna

Imperium Luminis. Empire of Light. I had first heard that name during the third day of my freshman year at Princeton—the same day that I unexpectedly crossed paths with Anna.

I was one of the first students that afternoon to enter the wood-paneled, book-lined classroom in East Pyne—a setting that photographers for official campus publications gravitated toward, so perfectly did the high, vaulted ceiling and leaded windowpanes connote refinement and scholarship. I was impressed to the point of intimidation. The classrooms at my old high school were dark and parochial, the desks covered with generations of graffiti. I took a seat at the gleaming mahogany table in East Pyne, wondering whether I, the son of a subway motorman, was truly ready for the transition to that courtly classroom. Would I be found out, or even give myself away through some obscure breach of conduct or decorum?

Charles Slagle, the Jacqueline V. Suppe Professor of Religious Studies, arrived and took the head of the table. Dark spots on his scalp showed through his thin white hair. A bushy mustache hooded his upper lip. With his shaking hands and unsteady gait and sunken cheeks, he looked weak and superannuated, well into a state of physical decline. He sat down and, while shuffling through his papers, began the course abruptly, almost confrontationally.

"Okay then," he said, squinting at us. "Who can define the word 'cult'?"

I did not want to risk offering definitions to the eminent Charles Slagle, whose own book was serving as the text for the course. I had signed up for the class solely because taking a course with Slagle had become mixed up in my mind with all that Princeton represented. When my father had pushed me to apply to Princeton, I ordered applications and brochures from the admissions office; and there, on the cover of one of the viewbooks, was Slagle's sagacious face staring out from behind a lectern, holding a small group of racially diverse students in rapt attention. I had only the vaguest notion of the nature of Gnostic cults, which were his area of expertise, but I resolved to be among those awestruck students in his class. I signed up for the only available seminar with him: "Sectarianism and Cults."

"I'm glad no one has an answer, at least not yet," he said. "What I want to have this semester is an open and extended discussion about cults. What are they? Who joins them? Are there characteristics we can consider to be held in common? Is it possible to differentiate them on an a priori basis from more accepted quote-unquote legitimate religious organizations?"

The door opened with a slow, haunted-house creak. Anna Barrett tip-toed into the room and mouthed the word "sorry" to Slagle. She proceeded into the classroom and froze when she saw me. I couldn't believe my bad luck. I knew Anna was coming to Princeton, of course, but with a thousand freshmen I thought my chances of crossing paths with her, at least so soon, were fairly remote. She represented all that I despised:

she was a spoiled rich girl who had gotten into Princeton on her stepfather's money and reputation. Carl Barrett was a big-time donor, so
there was never any doubt that Anna would end up at Princeton, but
she hadn't even had the decency to show up for her first class on time.

The only empty chair at the table was the one to my left, between me
and Slagle. Anna took the seat and opened a notebook, pointedly ignoring me.

After that I was useless. Slagle continued to discuss the early Christian
Church and the concept of heresy, but I was concentrating on my new
classmate. She was wearing a white silk shirt, just on the tantalizing
verge of translucency, and a knee-length skirt. When she crossed her
legs, her stockings emitted a soft staticky sound, reminding me that only
eight months before I had been permitted to run my hand over those
very legs, which remained long and maddeningly desirable. As much as
I affected disinterest, it seemed impossible that Anna was not listening
to the rhythm of my breathing, and from it suspecting my desire.

A sheet of paper slid in front of me on the table, pushed along by the
student on my right. A list labeled PRESENTATION TOPICS ran down its
left-hand side. Next to all but two topics were names written in various
handwritings and colors of ink. I gathered that the sheet had made its
way around the table and that Anna and I would be the last to choose.
The two remaining topics were "Justin the Gnostic" and "Imperium
Luminis."

I had no idea what either one signified or entailed. I chose Justin the
Gnostic.

As I read Anna's next e-mail, I wondered what would have happened
had I chosen differently. Is it possible that fate can be determined by
the precipitant action of a mind distracted by nylon stockings and familiar perfume?

Matt,

Here's the unvarnished truth about what happened after I left your place that afternoon. I was pretty angry at you. I thought my showing up would at least be a nice surprise, but I could clearly see that you hated me. I wrote you that note about how I was going to change everything. The truth is as soon as I left your place I said, fuck him what does he know? I went to one of the grungy bars on Queens Boulevard near your place and spent the rest of the afternoon drinking. I had nothing else to do. No job, no desire to see my stepfather, no obligations of any kind. All I had to do was get to my friend Nicole's place in Red Hook that evening, and until then it couldn't hurt to have a few drinks, especially since they would help me forget that you wanted absolutely nothing to do with me.

When I left the bar it was already dark. I was a little wobbly and disoriented, but feeling great. I was singing to myself. About a block from the entrance to the train station two guys came out from behind a parked van. They wanted to talk to me. I walked faster, but one guy was in front of me and he showed me a knife. Hundreds of people were speeding by in their cars on Queens Boulevard but we were hidden in the shadows of the subway overpass. They took me back between the cars and looked through my wallet. There was nothing to stop them from doing far worse. It seemed like it took a year for them to say, "Thanks, bitch," and run off with the money—euros and all. I don't know how long I stayed there leaning against that car. It was one of the worst moments of my life, standing there in the dark, shaking, totally alone. And the worst part, the crazy part, was that I wanted to go back to the bar and have another drink to steady myself, and the only reason I didn't was that they had taken everything but my Metrocard.

On the train I was in a strange mood. Something had been changed inside me and I could see the true nature of things. What I saw around me was ugly and sick and horrible. The car was dirty, gloomy. A man across from me was reading pornography and smiling to himself. I suspected that the other passengers were evil and corrupt in various ways: wife-beaters, adulterers, racists, child molesters. I never want to feel that way again. If you had told me that there was even one redeeming feature of the world or its inhabitants, in rebuttal I would have shown you the crazy man in Times Square screaming nonsense at the top of his lungs. Later that night he pushed a woman onto the tracks. I read about it the next day and it didn't surprise me. Of *course* someone was going to die a meaningless death at the hands of a madman that night. There was no logic, no protection, no comfort—just a pack of brutal animals wandering in their caverns.

When I got to Nicole's neighborhood, I was surprised that she lived in a desolate, industrial area. Her old place in Manhattan was a twenty-four-hours-a-day party (which was why I got in touch with her in the first place). I was shocked when I saw the state of her building. I assumed she'd had some terrible accident that made it impossible for her to earn money. When she opened the door I said, "What are you doing living in this shithole?" and she took a long look at me and said, "I'm very happy here. I think *you're* the one still living in a shithole." It was a slap in the face. I saw myself the way she saw me, drunk and pathetic and penniless, a total train-wreck of a human being. I hadn't painted anything meaningful in a year. I had no college degree. No prospects of any kind. Everyone I had ever known or loved hated me, most importantly you. And I just broke down, right there on this almost stranger's doorway. I sat on the floor and cried until her neighbors stuck their heads out their doors to see if anyone was hurt. She sat next to me and said, "Don't worry. There is a reason you came to see me tonight. You were brought here by God. I can help you. You are not alone."

I SERIOUSLY CONSIDERED dropping the Slagle class. I found it enervating to have to sit near Anna. After that first class, she had leisurely packed up her books, shouldered her bag and strolled out into the hallway, all without saying a word to me. Her arrogance and reserve left me in a state of embarrassed shock. Did I mean so little to her that I wasn't even worth acknowledging as a human being? She would have paid more attention to a vaguely familiar dog. I brooded over the incident for several days, at first deciding that I should take a different class to avoid repeated exposure to Anna, but finally concluding that I wouldn't be forced out of the class I had so looked forward to; I would not give her the satisfaction.

Besides, Slagle was turning out to be a mesmerizing teacher, and the subject—especially the obscure early Christian-era cults—had taken hold of my imagination. When the time came to prepare my presentation on Justin the Gnostic, I was fascinated by what I read.

According to Justin the Gnostic and his followers, there were three original, uncreated deities named Elohim, Eden and the Good. Elohim and Eden, who are ignorant of the existence of the Good, create Adam and Eve through a marriage union, and thus humans possess some soul from each of these deities. All is harmonious until Elohim discovers the higher realm of the Good. He remains there, abandoning Eden, who has no idea where her consort has gone. Angry over her abandonment, Eden directs her angels to introduce sexual desire and divorce and various sins to humankind. Elohim, in time, directs his messenger to appear to a twelve-year-old Nazarene named Jesus. The angel briefs Jesus on the true nature of the universe, and Jesus is commissioned to rectify the situation. When he is crucified, the part of the soul derived from Elohim ascends to the realm of the Good and there rejoins Elohim, while the part of the soul belonging to Eden remains behind with the body.

In my life until that point, there was God, there was the Son and there was the Holy Spirit, and either you believed or you didn't. There was no alternative cosmology. The story of Justin the Gnostic struck me as exciting and even seductive. It occurred to me that there was no more verifiable truth to the standard Christian story than there was to this wild myth. If a man in first-century Rome had turned down a different street one morning, if a mule in Macedonia had not brayed and interrupted his master, if Justin the Gnostic had been a more charismatic or convincing preacher, or if any one of a million other eventualities had occurred, then history could have proceeded differently. Justin the Gnostic's version of the universe would have triumphed, and his confused story would have struck me as coherent, majestic and ordinary.

Of course, I kept such reflections out of my presentation to the class. When I finished, Slagle nodded and said, "Palestine in the first centuries after Christ was crawling with self-proclaimed messiahs and prophets, many of them of the Gnostic variety. They were competing with the Christians for the souls of the world. They weren't lunatics, either, at least not all of them. Justin's creation myth is actually quite subtle and beautiful. Sin as the work of an abandoned deity. It has all the elements of the biblical stories, just rearranged and put together differently."

Anna was next. We had not spoken or even made eye contact in class, nor did we do so as I relinquished the floor. Rather than walking to the front of the room, where I had stood as I read my presentation, she lingered in the back and placed on the mahogany conference table a large black box. From her bag she extracted a thin laptop computer, which she connected to the box with a short cable. A shaft of bright white light shot out of the box and projected, on the far wall, a computer-generated slide with the words:

IMPERIUM LUMINIS:

AN EMPIRE OF LIGHT?

by Anna Damiani

I was so furious at her exhibition of this gadget that I didn't even register the unfamiliar last name until just before Anna changed the slide. I had worked diligently on my talk, and while it hardly broke new scholarly ground, it was clear and concise. I was being upstaged by a technological onslaught. The title words glowed in yellow on a soothing blue background, while Anna herself was dressed in a smart gray pantsuit that contributed to the professional demeanor. Slagle's eyes were widened in surprise and delight. Even before Anna opened her mouth, I knew that no one, least of all Professor Slagle, would look back on my talk as anything but a warm-up to this multimedia extravaganza.

"We've heard presentations about ancient and medieval heresies and sects," she began. "So when I signed up for the topic of Imperium Luminis I assumed it was another Gnostic cult. I was in for a surprise. It turns out that Imperium Luminis is a modern-day organization, a controversial branch of the Catholic Church."

At Anna's touch of a key on the computer, the title screen dissolved into a sea of pixels, which coalesced into the face of a man. He was stout and severe-looking, with a heavy brow and dark eyes; he had apparently been caught in the act of preaching, mouth open and hand raised with an air of charismatic authority.

"This is Giuseppe Conti, the founder of Imperium Luminis. He was born in Sicily in 1912 and was on his way to becoming a powerful local politician with ties to the Mafia until he underwent a conversion experience in his mid-twenties. He retreated to a hut in the interior of the island, where he had a vision of a new Catholic organization. This group would be composed not exclusively of priests and nuns, but also of ordinary people who wanted a closer relationship to God in their everyday lives."

She changed the slide, and a list of names came up, perhaps thirty or forty in all.

"Imperium Luminis has flourished in the past fifty years. This is a list of bishops and highly placed Vatican officials who are members of the group. It's an interesting case from the perspective of this class. Imperium Luminis is a recognized branch of the Catholic Church, but there are concerns about how the organization works. It concentrates on recruiting those who are troubled and depressed, often those who are addicted to drugs or alcohol, and then subjecting them to high-pressured 'Exercises.' Once in the group, members submit to close control by priests who keep track of all aspects of the members' lives, even approving which books members can read. Critical inquiry is discouraged. Strict obedience is demanded."

I was surprised that I had never heard of Imperium Luminis, since I had been raised as a Catholic. But I was much more interested in Anna herself than in what she was saying about this fanatical group. She spoke with confidence and poise; through extensive study, innate intelligence or both, she had achieved a mastery of the subject matter. It was possible to believe that she was a guest lecturer from the Religion department. She salted the talk with fantastic words—*exegetical, syncretism, eschatological*. She looked beautiful, too, with her long dark hair shining in the light from the projector and her lithe body leaning over the table as she consulted her notes. I snapped back to attention when she reached her conclusion and, for some reason, looked directly at me.

"Imperium Luminis bears some similarities to the other sects we've been studying, but these comparisons only go so far. Imperium Luminis is an organization in good standing within the Catholic Church. The Pope is a supporter, and Giuseppe Conti is expected to be canonized within a few years. In other words, this is not a straightforward case of a freestanding cult, but rather an instance of similar behaviors arising within an orthodox context. Perhaps, then, we should consider the extremist groups we've been studying as the products of some more universal human tendency."

Slagle closed his eyes as though savoring fine wine.

"Ahh, superb," he said and began to clap, with the rest of the class following his lead. They had not clapped for me. Anna looked down at the table and smiled slightly, embarrassed by her brilliance. For all my anger at being upstaged and all my resentment of Anna in general, I couldn't help but be impressed.

On the way out of the classroom I found myself next to her. I thought it would be poor sportsmanship not to acknowledge her.

"Hey, great job," I said.

I was puzzled by the expression on her face, which was not arrogant or disdainful, but something closer to frightened.

"Thanks. You too," she said, and hurried out of the room.

If you had told me when I visited you that within a few months I would be a novice in the Light, I would never have believed you. But Nicole told me that she could help me and revealed the truths of Imperium Luminis. My old fears and needs began to fall away. I felt an overwhelming relief, a sense of peace that made me cry for hours and hours. I had wanted some way out of the life I had made for myself and the mistakes I had made, and I was being given a second chance by God. Nicole brought me right away to the Imperium Luminis house, and I spent most of that night talking to Father Harrington, who made me understand amazing things about myself and about life. It's been a long and difficult period of searching and questioning, but I feel at peace here. I've finished a long journey and now I can rest. I see that everything up until this moment has been part of God's plan for me, and I'm willing to follow His direction for the future.

This is the best thing that has ever happened to me, and I really want to see you again to share my new life with you. I got the sense when I visited you that I wasn't the only one who was unhappy. You seemed a little lonely, a little listless. Can't we forget about the past few years and be friends again? I think in the end we both need each other.

And, by the way, Imperium Luminis is *not* a cult. I was totally, completely wrong in Slagle's class. I had gotten all that information from very biased sources. Take the issue of censorship. I'm here because I want to live as holy a life as possible. Is it so strange that I would talk to a priest about various aspects of what I'm doing and thinking? I might say, "I'm reading such and such a book," and he would say, "Fine, but you should be aware that we believe the book is wrong for such and such a reason." This happened the other day when Father Harrington saw that I was reading a Horace Jacob Little book. He showed me an essay Horace Jacob Little had written disparaging the existence of God, and suddenly I saw what I was reading in a new light. That's all. It's a matter of being aware of potential biases and untruths, of having the most information possible.

And all the rest of the issues that I brought up in Slagle's class are in reality just as harmless.

It would be so much easier to talk to you about this and everything else face-to-face! So why don't we get together sometime?

DURING THAT FIRST SEMESTER, my roommate was taking a studio art class. Having nothing better to do one Wednesday evening, I accompanied him to a reception celebrating an exhibition of student artwork. He promised free alcohol, and I was disappointed to find only soda and apple juice and dry crackers with pretentious cheese.

As I scanned the room and examined the mostly unremarkable paintings and sketches, my eyes were arrested by a large painting on the far wall. It showed, in vague shadows as through a heavy fog, a man walking into the foreground of the painting. He carried himself heavily, seemingly exhausted, and he was looking backward with a complex expression of disgust and disappointment and regret. I wandered closer to the painting. The technique was a heavy impasto, with smears of gray and black and blue that lent a tortured quality to the scene. The face of the man was riveting, skillfully rendered, brimming with identifiable emotion. The painting was surrounded by ham-handed still lifes, and the effect was as though someone had hung a masterpiece from the campus art museum among the work of kindergartners.

I looked at the tag, which said:

INTO EXILE

Anna Damiani

Oil on canvas

I looked around and, sure enough, there she was, across the room, sipping soda and talking to a group of fellow students. I watched her for a few minutes, equally desirous and contemptuous, until finally her eyes wandered away from her companions and caught mine. An expression of distress flickered across her face. She quickly looked away into space.

I waited until the conversation broke up and she was alone. I was going to put a stop to this contest of avoidance we had been conducting.

"Hi, I'm Matt Kelly," I said, in a voice of sarcastic amiability, pretending she should have no idea who I was.

She regarded me suspiciously for a second, then extended her hand and said, playing along, "Anna Damiani. Nice to meet you."

"You look amazingly like someone I used to know—Anna Barrett."

"I know her. A total snob, in my opinion. She once told me about something awful she did. She went out a few times with this great guy who she was very interested in, but unfortunately his family didn't have much money. He had a little too much of a New York accent, if you know what I mean. And the Barretts, as I'm sure you know, are loaded. Anyway, her parents insisted that she stop seeing this guy, and she didn't have the guts to stand up to them even though she wanted to. So she just broke off the relationship. She was too embarrassed to even tell him why."

"He knew why."

When Anna had stopped seeing me in high school I was upset—not because I was losing her (we had only just met) but because I knew I had been deemed unfit to associate with her. The rejection stung to the point that I began to be embarrassed by my family's house and clothes and general level of refinement. Every time our old vibrating hulk of a Chevy stalled at a red light, I thought, *You see? That's why Anna Barrett won't go out with you.*

"I owe you an apology," she said. "I've been trying to avoid you because I thought you would never want to talk to me. I'm ashamed that I didn't stand up to my parents."

"What's with the new last name?"

"It's my biological father's name. I'm dropping Barrett. It's symbolic. I'm tired of my mother and my stepfather trying to control my life. The thing with you was actually the last straw. And, of course, they don't want me to be an artist."

"But they're still paying your tuition, right?"

"Actually, no. I applied as Anna Damiani and listed my biological father on the application. He's paying."

I must have done a poor job of hiding my utter astonishment, because she smiled and looked at the floor to hide her amusement.

"I can paint what I want," she said, waving at her painting. "See who I want."

She raised her eyebrows to indicate that the last words were a tentative invitation. I looked at the painting and said, "I'm genuinely impressed."

"It's Adam. Being expelled from the Garden. I'm reading *Paradise*

Lost for an English class. For some reason I just saw the scene this way and I wanted to paint it."

The reception was breaking up. We were among the stragglers.

"What are you doing now?" I said. "How about we go get some coffee?"

That was the first day that I truly began to understand Anna. I suspected that despite the name change the admission staff had nevertheless identified her as the stepdaughter of a generous donor and admitted her partly on that basis. Even so, to do what she had done—to reject even ceremonially the benefit of the Barrett name—took passion, courage and a degree of lunacy, all of which I found admirable. She was a free spirit, which was why her later acceptance of the strict rules and limitations of Imperium Luminis was so uncharacteristic. Anna had never wanted to be ruled by anyone, but she ended up giving over her autonomy completely, the burden of it being far greater than she anticipated.

At the time, the subject matter of her painting—a stylized Adam staggering out of the Garden, strangely enough without Eve—seemed simply a backdrop to the real drama, which was our conversation and reconciliation. But looking back, I wondered whether there wasn't a deeper significance to the painting. There was apparently something in her mind that was fundamentally attracted to a biblical scene. No other student had thought to depict prophets or saints or plagues or floods. Her painting was about the rage of God at the disobedience of humans, about punishment for a fall from grace. And what else, after all, was her time with Imperium Luminis?

THREE

ON THE SECOND to last day of the schoolyear, with all my teaching and lessons finished and only final grading and paperwork separating me and the freedom of the summer, I took the subway down to the Imperium Luminis house to see Anna. It was the day after I had received her e-mailed invitation, and I wanted to waste no time in investigating her new circumstances.

I found myself on a No. 9 train at the hands of a malevolent or inexperienced motorman. The train shook and lurched disgracefully down the tracks. I always noticed the motorman's performance. For all the embarrassment that my father's blue-collar profession had caused me at Princeton, I couldn't help but feel a small thrill of excitement whenever I rode the train. I had been raised on and around the subways. One of my earliest memories is of my father explaining to me how the signals worked. My fifth-grade science project was on the interlocking system, which keeps switches and signals from being set against each other. I knew how to drive the train, too—several times, my father had let me work the controls of an empty train in the yard before one of his runs. "The passenger should be able to stand perfectly balanced for the entire ride without touching a strap or pole," he would say. Accomplishing this required a soft hand on the throttle, a gentle touch on the brake. I took these lessons seriously, imagining that someday I might be called upon to operate a subway train. It offended my sensibilities to encounter someone performing as ineptly as the motorman did on that No. 9 train, alternating between excessive speed and sharp braking, repeatedly throwing everyone off balance.

As I fought for equilibrium, watching the ghostly reflection of the car's interior in the dark window, I tried to imagine what I would discover at the Imperium Luminis house. In a perfect world, I would find Anna much as she was back in the early days of our relationship, before everything went out of control. But I was skeptical of her supposed transformation. Having just regained my direction after losing her once, I wanted at all costs to avoid a repetition.

The Village was its usual self, a mixture of chipper NYU students and yuppies and women with pythons around their necks. I turned off Bleecker and down a quiet, tree-lined street that the rest of the neighborhood seemed to have overlooked, allowing it to sneak unchanged into the modern city. Traffic was scant and flowers sprouted from windowboxes on the sills of handsome brick townhouses. A patch of pavement near the curb had been worn away, revealing ancient cobblestones and a single rail from an otherwise obliterated trolley track.

The address brought me to a townhouse of red brick with a black door at the top of a flight of stairs. In my past experience I had found that most locations of official Catholic capacity in the city were dark, hoary places adjacent to churches. Instead, this was a distinguished nineteenth-century residence with not a church in sight. It seemed to be an expensive private home. There was no sign identifying it as belonging to Imperium Luminis. Uncertain whether I was in the right place and expecting to annoy whatever homeowner answered the door, I rang the bell. A female voice came over the intercom box and said, "Could you please take a step backward?"

A security camera above the door whirred as it swiveled and focused on me.

"Do you have an appointment?"

"I think there may be a mistake. Can you just tell me if this is the Imperium Luminis building?"

"Who is it you want to see?"

"Anna Damiani."

Several minutes passed. I watched a tired-looking man pushing a baby stroller down the street. A car coasted down the block and slowed as it neared a fire hydrant, then sped up—looking for a parking space. A male pigeon strutted and cooed in the vicinity of a disinterested female. Either there was great confusion within the building about whether or not I should be admitted, or they had forgotten me. I was about to ring the buzzer again to remind them I was waiting when the black door opened.

Instead of Anna, a tall man appeared in the doorway. He wore tan slacks and a white dress shirt. His hair was mostly gray. His shoulders were broad and he stood ramrod straight, giving him a soldierly demeanor.

"I'm looking for Imperium Luminis," I said.

"I'm Father Harrington." His voice was soothing and effortlessly deep, the voice of an orator at rest. "It's good to meet you, Matt."

Something about the way he spoke, the way his gaze locked into my eyes and did not waver, made me uncomfortable. I got the impression that he was evaluating me in light of previously formed opinions, and I found it presumptuous that he had called me by my name before I told it to him.

Harrington showed me to his office, which was on the first floor near the entrance. It was a dark study with two windows that gave onto the street at tree level. An Oriental carpet of deep reds and purples covered the floor. The bookshelves, which had doors of glass, were filled with titles containing the words "Giuseppe Conti" and "Imperium Luminis" and other phrases that I could barely translate with my vestigial Latin. Two leather wingback chairs sat before a large desk that was set at an angle to the rest of the room. A sleek laptop and a slim telephone were the only objects on the desk.

"So tell me about yourself," Harrington said, inviting me to sit. He perched on the front edge of his desk, directly in front of me.

"Really, I'm just here to say hello to Anna."

He shook his head. "I'm afraid you can't just pop in here and expect to see someone. We're not a hotel."

My first impulse was to argue this premise. I couldn't imagine that Anna, fiercely independent Anna, would approve of this limitation of her freedom. Did Harrington intend to turn me away if I did not pass muster?

"What do you know about Imperium Luminis?" he said.

"I've heard of Giuseppe Conti."

"There's quite a lot of misinformation out there about our group. I'd like to make sure you know the truth." He took a deep breath and looked down, seeming to consider how best to reduce the essentials of Imperium Luminis to a few words. "Imperium Luminis is an organization dedicated to the proposition that you don't need to be a priest or a nun to become closer to God. There are a few priests who help to administer and run the group. But the vast majority of our members are ordinary Catholics who have jobs and families. They join because they're troubled by the tenor and content of our secular culture, and because they're dissatisfied with the anemic worship that takes place in the local parishes. We are the Marine Corps of the Catholic Church. Our members are a spiritual elite, strong and united in their faith."

He stopped and regarded me warily. He appeared to expect an argument from me.

"Do you believe in God, Matt?" he said.

"Sure."

He scowled.

"That's not the kind of question you can answer in a casual way. I didn't ask you if you wanted a slice of pizza. I said, do you believe in God, and if you *do,* I would expect to hear something more resounding."

I was on the verge of making a more vehement declaration when something stopped me. Maybe it was the feeling that I was being manipulated, or maybe it was simply that at the deepest level I could not make such an affirmation truthfully. Harrington waited for me to say something. When I remained silent, he said, "I don't think Anna is available to see you."

He extended one hand toward the door, palm facing the ceiling. Shocked and confused, I had no choice but to stand and begin a slow walk to the door, all the while wondering what exactly I was doing.

How could I see Anna if not with his permission? And why wouldn't I simply say what he wanted to hear? Just as I touched the knob, Harrington spoke.

"You go out with Anna for three years. By her report, you two are inseparable. You are too young then, of course, but thoughts of marriage certainly occur to you. Then everything goes wrong. Something changes inside her, and suddenly she is unrecognizable to you, unrecognizable even to herself. You spend a year missing her, wondering if there can be any hope of going back to the way things used to be. Finally, just when you've given up, she's back. From all appearances she is better. She invites you to see her. You come down here. And after all that, you would be turned away so easily by a priest who asks you a simple question about God?"

He looked at me with professional scrutiny.

"What difference does it make?" I said. "I'm just visiting her."

"My primary concern is Anna's spiritual health. If I think your influence would detract from it, I will be much less enthusiastic about letting you see her. And, by the way, you're not just 'visiting' her. There's no doubt in my mind that she wants to invite you back into her life."

"And she would have no problem letting you decide this for her?"

"Of course not."

There was a maliciousness in Harrington's insistence on my stating a belief in God, as when children are fighting and the stronger forces the weaker to cry uncle. I was beginning to piece together an idea of how Imperium Luminis operated, how Anna's new life was organized and constrained.

"I was raised Catholic," I said. "I believe in God."

He looked me over and sighed. Glancing behind me toward the doorway, he said, "Ah—here she is."

I did not register the fact that Anna had appeared at the exact moment of his acquiescence, suggesting that the whole encounter was choreographed and that Anna's cue was some signal from Harrington that I had failed to notice. I did not reflect on Harrington's demand for a confession of faith and what that said about Imperium Luminis. My attention was entirely focused on Anna herself, standing in the doorway with her arms clasped demurely behind her. She wore a long floral-print dress. Her hair, which had been returned to its natural copper color, was tamed into a neat ponytail. She looked entirely different from the Anna who had arrived at my apartment in the rain. That Anna had been world-weary, chain-smoking, examining everything with jumpy, mournful eyes. Now she smiled when I saw her and opened her eyes a little wider, unable to entirely control her excitement.

"We'll talk again soon," Harrington said to me as I walked toward Anna, but I could barely acknowledge him. If I had let my eyes wander from her she might have stopped looking at me with that giddy, expectant expression.

I followed her to a parlor with formal couches and a shiny coffee table. The room was separated from the hallway only by a low wall and a set of pillars. It struck me as a very public place for a confidential discussion. We sat on the same couch, sitting halfway off the cushions to face each other, our knees in close proximity.

"How are you?" I said.

"I'm happy. Everything makes sense now. I've been able to do a lot of thinking here, about us. I was always looking for something and now I've found it. I actually wish we could be meeting for the first time, now that I have my priorities straight."

"What are your priorities?"

"Love of God, discipline of the self and devotion to the Benefactor."

"The Benefactor?"

"It's a term of respect for Giuseppe Conti. Bottom line is I don't need to get high or drunk anymore. I'm ready to experience life as a normal person. Every day I get up and it's like I've been let out of prison. Have you ever walked around the city and just thought life is wonderful and perfect?"

She smiled and leaned back into the couch. The overwhelming impression was of someone well-scrubbed. Her floral dress would have been appropriate for a garden party at the Barrett estate in Montauk. There was a glow about her, a vitality and serenity, that I had not seen since the first days we were together.

"Have you been painting much?" I said.

"I'm not going to paint anymore. It's discouraged here. As the Benefactor says, 'You must make yourself indifferent to all created things.'"

"So that's it? Your life's ambition?"

"It was the wrong path. I can see that now. I was painting because I wanted to be famous. I wanted people to look at the work in some distant museum and say, *Ah, what genius!* It was an exercise in vanity."

"What are you going to do instead?"

"I'm working as an editorial assistant at a magazine."

Father Harrington walked down the hallway next to us, well within earshot. The room, and the building as a whole, felt confining and close.

"Just tell me what the ultimate goal is here."

"The ultimate goal is salvation. I've already moved out into my own place in Alphabet City. I'm starting a new life. But I'll always be a member of the Light. I owe everything to them."

"Does your stepfather know about this?"

"I told him. He's finding it hard to understand."

I glanced down the hallway and lowered my voice to a whisper. "This Father Harrington wasn't going to let me see you if I said I didn't believe in God."

She shrugged.

"He would have. He was just testing you a little."

She put her hand on mine.

"I really think we should see each other more. I think we deserve another chance."

I had wished so often to hear her say those words. Of course, I had envisioned her saying them in an artist's studio somewhere, surrounded by canvases and paint and the assorted junk she always accumulated wherever she worked; but how could I object that things were not exactly as I had imagined? I wanted to say yes. I wanted to take hold of her, to let her rest her head on my shoulder, just as she used to.

"All this," I said, waving to indicate Imperium Luminis as a whole, "is a little bit much."

"What do you mean?"

"Priests telling you what to do, who you can and can't see. Where is this all coming from?"

She looked puzzled and a little panicked. It seemed she had not expected my objection and could not make sense of it.

"I've never been so sure that something is right. I've found the best way to live. My life has been directly affected by God. I know it at a basic level. I know it the way I know up from down."

"I'm worried that they've . . ." I could not even say the word, so ridiculous did it sound. But how else to explain the situation?

"What? Indoctrinated me? *Brainwashed* me?"

I nodded.

Sudden anger flashed in her eyes, which I took as a positive sign. Anna was by nature passionate, and a look of defiance suited her far better than the beatific manner she had adopted at Imperium Luminis. It was her passion, I thought, that must have been responsible for her joining Imperium Luminis in the first place. She had decided to turn away from illicit habits—and, true to form, she had done so in the most exuberant and extreme manner possible.

"First of all, let me remind you that this is a Catholic organization endorsed—no, not just endorsed, *championed*—by the Pope himself. This is not the Moonies or the Branch Davidians. And second, how about giving me a little more credit than to assume I could be hypnotized into obedience? What is this, *The Manchurian Candidate?*"

Articulate indignation was vintage Anna. I wondered whether I was making too much of Imperium Luminis. Maybe I should just be grateful that she was sober and happy and even willing to pick up where we left off.

A bell rang and Anna stood.

"I've got to go now," she said, and kissed me on the cheek. She gave me a piece of paper and said, "Come see me." She hurried out of the room without looking back.

The paper contained Anna's address and phone number. I slipped it into my pocket. It occurred to me that I would very much like to meet Anna at her new place, where we might be able to speak more freely about Imperium Luminis and how she had decided to become a member.

On my way out the door, Harrington's secretary waylaid me and pressed upon me a paperback copy of *The Pilgrim,* by Giuseppe Conti. I told her I didn't want it, but she insisted that I take it.

The front cover of the book depicted the hut in the Sicilian countryside, atop a mountain by the sea, where Giuseppe Conti had received his vision of Imperium Luminis. In the picture on the cover, the hut and the landscape were shrouded in darkness while the sky above was a daytime sky, pale blue with serene white clouds. I found the picture surreal and vaguely unsettling. Was the day lording it over the night, or was the night encroaching on the day? The mismatch mirrored my disorientation upon leaving the Imperium Luminis house. All my prayers had apparently been answered, my hopes fulfilled. Anna was on the verge of returning to my life. But on closer examination, the strange elements of the scene did not correspond to any reality I had anticipated or desired.

I turned to the blurb on the back cover of *The Pilgrim* and read,

This is the story of a life begun in the prison of corruption and completed in the light of hope and faith. This is the autobiographical account of how redemption came to one lost sinner, and how he founded the movement that has called hundreds of thousands of ordinary Catholics to live more holy lives, revitalizing the Church and sanctifying the world. This is the story of Giuseppe Conti and the Empire of Light.

FOUR

O N   T H E   S U B W A Y out to Queens from the Imperium Luminis
house, I began to leaf through *The Pilgrim,* hoping to find in it some
indication of the purpose and scope of Imperium Luminis. My parents
had invited me over for dinner that night, and sitting in the living room
of the house where I grew up, as the smell of browning onions drifted in
from the kitchen, I started to read it in earnest:

*I was entirely in love with the body and the pleasures of the flesh, yet I
found nothing meaningful and everything absurd. I was sick of living and
terrified of death.*

Where would I be, O Lord, had You not taken pity on me and restored me to myself? What further miseries would I have suffered? What fears endured, a child lost in the night? Surely I would have taken my own life, either inadvertently or with premeditation, for what purpose does the world serve, and why would one wish to linger in it, when one does not recognize Your sustaining presence?

I can say with confidence that my very earliest thoughts betrayed my innate ignorance and sinfulness. What, after all, is an infant capable of but want and desire? The specifics of my thought are lost to me, but not to You, O Lord, who hold all of the past and the future in Your infinite mind. Certainly it was something like this: my dear nurse Maria holding me on her knee, bouncing me up and down, feeding me spoonfuls of mashed fruit, and I—with the miracle of consciousness dawning over my hitherto useless brain—gazing greedily at the bowl of fruit, thinking (for the first time, thinking!), I want more, I want more and more and more.

How does the bird decide how high to fly? Is it not the tendency of all living things to escape the earth, to rise, to soar? O Lord, what an earthbound creature I was—a snake, a mole, a burrowing insect hiding from the light. Your Word has lifted me up, and through these words, may yet lift others!

—"*The Pilgrim?*" my father said, coming into the room. "I'm surprised to see you reading that."

He opened a beer and sat heavily on the rickety sofa, which creaked at the introduction of the burden. He was wearing his uniform from work.

"You've heard of Giuseppe Conti?" I said. If my parents knew anything about Imperium Luminis, they had certainly never discussed it with me.

"Sure. The founder of Imperium Luminis."

He switched on the television and flipped through the channels until he found the Yankees game. When he saw the score, Yanks down by three in the eighth, he grunted and scowled. The banter of the commentators washed over us, a litany of statements of the count— . . . *and the one-two, way outside, now two-and-two* . . . —that was as steady the ticking of a clock.

"So why are you reading it?" he said when a commercial came on.

"Curiosity."

"I figured as much."

"What do you mean by that?"

"I presume you're not reading *The Pilgrim* for its spiritual insights. You're reading it so you can feel superior to the gullible believers of the world."

I was reluctant to say anything further because we were approaching perilous territory. My father and I did not see eye to eye on matters of religion. My father was a devout and exemplary Catholic. When I was young he did his best to attend Mass every morning on his way to work—just him and a scattering of blue-haired retirees in the pews. I myself received the sacraments, dutifully and even enthusiastically. I went to Catholic school right up until Princeton. But during Thanksgiving break in my freshman year, my parents asked me what I was working on at school. Quite innocently, I told them about the paper I was writing for Slagle's class on Justin the Gnostic.

"And what does Justin the Gnostic believe?" my mother said.

I told them the whole, fantastical story of the creation according to Justin—Elohim, Eden and the angels commissioning Jesus to save the world.

"That's ridiculous," my father said. "Why are you wasting your time with nonsense? Did you really go to Princeton to study heresies?"

"It's only a heresy because Justin the Gnostic didn't win in the end."

"This Justin the Gnostic didn't win *because* he was wrong," my father said, lowering his voice as he did when he no longer wished to be contradicted. I proceeded, surprisingly pleased with the reaction I was producing:

"Maybe it's all an accident of history, and we believe what we do because it's a good story that gets handed down again and again. Maybe it's all a fairy tale and that's all there is to it."

My father shook his head and remained silent for a moment, before exploding:

"What good is this going to do you? It's only going to bring you pain and confusion. Drop this stupid class and don't think about this again. Just trust me on this. Don't turn your back on God."

I did not drop the class, and over the next several years I took up a running argument with my father over God and religion. What was it, after all, that had allowed my father—in his own right a well-read, intelligent and capable man who had graduated with honors from Columbia before he was drafted to Vietnam—to persist for twenty-five years in the job of subway motorman, driving an endless succession of trains through the dismal tunnels of the city? What had kept him from going on to graduate school or becoming, say, a Carl H. Barrett? It was a great puzzle to me how all traces of ambition seemed to have been eradicated from his life. I blamed it on the influence of the Church, which had taught him to be humble, to accept his blue-collar lot, to be thankful for what he had and not strive for better. I wasn't about to allow myself to be constrained in the same way. Anna and I were going to be free of the old superstitions of our ancestors.

Inevitably, my father and I would argue whenever we got together. Once I said to him:

"If I told a psychiatrist that you believed someone was watching you twenty-four hours a day, noting down all your failures and sins; that the entire world was organized in some grand plan; that there were no coincidences; that every single thing that happened to you was directed by an outside intelligence—do you know what that psychiatrist would do? He'd have you locked up as a paranoid lunatic. It's a kind of madness."

He turned ashen and I believed that I had provoked him to some kind of unprecedented anger. But he wasn't angry.

"Don't ever talk about shrinks to me again," he said quietly, though for some reason clearly shaken, and he left the room.

Our discussions became more philosophical.

"You're so strident," he would say. "You act like you're the first free-thinker the world has ever seen. People have fought these battles before you, and you know what? People still believe. People will *always* believe. You're struggling against human nature."

There was a sadness in his voice when we discussed religion. I knew that this—in addition to my decision to join Teach for Humanity after graduation—was a reason he was disappointed in me.

The Yankees scored a run but left two stranded. At the next commercial I put down my copy of *The Pilgrim* and said, "What do you think of Imperium Luminis?"

My father regarded me as though he would rather not open another round of dialogue on religious matters.

"Why?"

"Anna Damiani's been back in touch with me. She's a member of Imperium Luminis now."

He made a prolonged whistling sound, indicating that this news was far beyond his ability to have foreseen it.

"And you think this is terrible?" he said.

"Actually, I'm not sure yet. It might be better than her drinking all the time."

"I don't know very much about Imperium Luminis. They're a pretty extreme group and a lot of people don't support them. But they're a part of the Church and on that level I accept them."

"But you would never join them."

"No," he chuckled. "Even I'm not *that* much of a believer."

I turned back to *The Pilgrim*, but before I could resume my reading my father said, "By the way, have you given any thought to what you want to do next year?"

"I might teach for another year. I really enjoy it."

He exhaled and shook his head.

"You know, you didn't have to go to Princeton to become a teacher at some rinky-dink public school in Harlem."

I was not in the mood to resume what had become a perpetual, inconclusive discussion about my future, so I did not say what was, to my mind, so obvious as to be almost comically ironic. Here was my father, who had himself forsaken all opportunities to get ahead in the world, lecturing *me* about *my* obligation to apply myself more diligently. I knew he only meant the best for me, but it absolutely infuriated me.

I kept silent and turned back to the book.

There is no peace but through reflection and self-discipline, just as there is no redemption but through Your gift of Grace. And how far removed I was from any of these qualities! It was simultaneously my blessing and my burden to be born in the land of Sicily—a blessing because here on this flowering, ravishing island it is indisputable that the external world is a gift from God, and a burden because here the most atrocious sins of mankind are so numerous and inescapable.

My family was an old and infamous one, with a name that can be found even in medieval texts, always spoken in a tone of fear—The Conti Family. How this situation arose is beyond the scope of my own humble story, and I hesitate to mention this background for fear my reader will think I am puffing myself up with self-importance. This could not be further from the truth. I am greatly ashamed of my family, a gang of thieves and murderers extending back for generations and generations. Just as Abraham reached a covenant with God, so must some unnamed ancestor of mine have concluded a bargain with the enemy of mankind, the trickster. The Contis were based in the southwestern portion of the island, and although we never spoke of such things, many people have since identified my family with the criminals who exert silent control over the island. What else could explain the gift that I received from my father at the tender age of ten? I remember his severe expression and gruff handshake as he handed me the package. How greedily and wantonly I unwrapped the tissue paper (for I had been nurtured in a spirit of indulgence and avarice, and nothing had countered my natural inclination toward sinfulness). I guessed that the package would contain candies, and I could almost taste them as I tore the covering to shreds. Instead, I was disappointed to find a book. It was Machiavelli's The Prince, *and inside, my father had written in dedication:*

To My Prince,
Read this book and learn its lessons well.

I did learn those lessons. Nothing was denied me, and I believed that nothing should be denied. I roamed my little world like an emperor, taking whatever I wished. As a teenager, I would walk through the streets of Sciacca pointing at the goods displayed in windows, and the servile merchants would send the items to my family's home without charge, as gifts to the Contis. If you had accused me of stealing I would have been shocked and outraged; and yet what else could it be called? When the fires of sexual desire began to rage I did not know the sting of rejection and humiliation, for who would deny the wishes of the son of the Contis, who was himself destined to assume power within a few years? Can it be said that I took advantage to the fullest? It can, O Lord, it can; and in the register of my sins that stretches for thousands of pages, without doubt the most vile and disgraceful charges relate to those girls of whom I took advantage. A teenage monster, ready to make the world monstrous! I hang my head in shame and freely admit to You, O Lord, that I have no right to forgiveness—no right even to speak Your name, but that You have commanded me to do so!

I was interrupted by the breaking of glass, as my father's bottle of beer shattered on the floor. I glanced up from *The Pilgrim*, expecting to see him leaping to his feet and swearing mildly at his clumsiness. He simply sat there, staring with an odd, searching expression at the remnants of the bottle on the floor, as if trying to discern some message in the pattern of foam and glass shards.

"Are you okay?" I said as a joke, and repeated the question in earnest when he did not answer. I thought he was so upset by a home run just surrendered by the Yankees that he would not reply. I noticed that his right hand was shaking—not a tremor of old age, but a genuine convulsing. He could not control it. He looked at me in alarm and grasped his right hand with his left, which was still working properly.

"Get your mother," he said.

I ran into the kitchen, where my mother was chopping carrots. When we went back into the living room I saw that his right leg was twitching, and his right shoulder as well.

"Not again," my mother said, throwing herself on the couch beside him and holding him around the neck to brace him.

"Again?" I said. "What the fuck is going on?"

The TV was blaring a car commercial. *But these deals won't last! Hurry hurry hurry in now!*

My father inhaled deeply and arched his back, looking up at the ceiling.

As I dialed the phone and went through the information with the 911 operator, I watched my father. He was unconscious, in the grip of a full-blown seizure, contracting and relaxing all his muscles in a tortured rhythm. My mother could not keep him on the couch, and the two of them fell to the ground with a thud. Instantly, blood spread across the floor. My father's frenzied arm had been sliced open by the glass shards.

Here is what the paramedics saw when they arrived: a burly, middle-aged man lying motionless on a living-room floor, the fit of the seizure having passed; his wife, weeping quietly and cradling his head; his son, pressing a kitchen towel soaked with blood to his arm; and a mixture of glass, beer and blood coating the floor around them.

"Did someone *stab* him?" the first paramedic said. He thought he had arrived on a crime scene. My mother and I both began to explain at once, and the paramedic's eyes flicked back and forth between us before he was able to make out that the patient had had a seizure.

"Does he have epilepsy? No? Any other health problems? Any medications he takes?"

The TV was on, replaying the highlights of the completed game. *And that one is going to roll all the way to the wall—will they send him? Here's the play at the plate: he is—*

I switched it off and, from a distance, watched them go to work.

MY FATHER was deeply and profoundly asleep in the hospital bed. The doctor in the emergency room had told us that this level of stupor was common after seizures. When we shook my father into awareness and asked him questions he would answer in a slurred voice and then his eyes would flicker shut, returning him to the underworld where his brain was recovering from its activity.

My mother was asleep in the chair to the right of my father's bed, her head bent backward and tilted toward one shoulder. It was the middle of the night and the room was dark. All that disturbed the silence was the intermittent trilling of a machine attached to my father's IV line. I went to look out the window. A light rain was falling, blurring the lights of the city and sounding a soft patter on the pane. There was no traffic on the street below; it was one of those moments when, in the depth of the night, it seems that you alone in the city are awake—a time of loosely connected thoughts and undisciplined memories.

"Don't let him die," my mother had said, grasping the arm of the paramedic.

"Don't worry," he said. "People usually don't die of seizures."

I remembered the night that Anna showed up at my apartment—it was raining then too. She had said something about watching the city as her plane circled over JFK, how the blurred orange and yellow lights somehow made her think of me. At the time I dismissed this as a strange, almost haphazard excuse for barging in on me, but as I gazed over the shiny streets and the faraway lights of Manhattan I thought I understood what she had meant: she felt lonely and small and lost, and she wanted to be with someone.

In the emergency room I had expected to find chaos and hyperactivity, as in the TV shows in which doctors and nurses bark orders and numbers as they circle inert patients. But once they determined that my father was conscious and that the bleeding from his arm had slowed, he became a low priority. We waited in a small examination room with nothing on the walls, my father already asleep and my mother simply staring straight ahead.

"Lots of people have epilepsy," I said. "It's not such a big deal."

She nodded and murmured an assent.

I could hear activity next door. Someone had swallowed some pills in a suicide attempt. There was a violent retching as the contents of the stomach came up. Someone was crying and saying, "How could you do this? *How* could you do this?"

A doctor came to see us, a man with an Indian accent who put his hand on my father's shoulder as he introduced himself. He asked the routine questions—medical history, past surgeries—and my mother answered for him. But when he asked about any hospitalizations, I was surprised to hear my father say, "Yes. One."

"What was that for?"

"At the VA hospital on Long Island."

The doctor looked up from his chart and said, "Yes, but what was the reason for the hospitalization?"

This was all news to me, and I assumed that his answer was the product of his confusion and exhaustion. I waited for my mother to correct him but she remained silent.

"It was psychiatric. I had some problems after the war," my father said with his eyes closed, and trailed off, returning to his dream. "Couldn't adjust . . ."

My family did not operate by hiding things—that was for other, more complicated families, like the Damiani/Barrett clan. And yet hadn't my parents also kept secret the fact that my father had had a smaller seizure a week before this big one? What else were they hiding? And what did it mean to be hospitalized on a psychiatric ward for "problems adjusting"? I asked my mother about it after the doctor left, but she said only, "Not right now." I was catching a glimpse of the person my father used to be, and the possibility that he could have been different, that he could have been weaker or troubled in some profound way, unsettled me to the core.

I had brought along my copy of *The Pilgrim,* and I switched on a small light to read, hoping for distraction. Giuseppe Conti detailed his continuing decline into corruption—which included ordering the assassination of a political rival—but aside from a general astonishment that the man was now on the road to sainthood, I could not summon the interest to continue reading for more than a few sentences. My father's breathing was steady and slow, and I watched his chest rise and fall for a while. The adventures of Giuseppe Conti seemed distant and irrelevant. Noticing a small spot of my father's blood on the back of the book, I tore the back cover off and crumpled it in my hand. The last few pages came off with it.

Toward midnight a neurologist appeared. He wore a bow tie and spoke in a nasal voice. My father was awake and professed to be feeling spectacular after his rest.

The doctor sat on the side of the bed and said, "The question that we needed to answer was, what caused this seizure? Unfortunately we found the answer. There is an abnormal mass on the left side of your brain. We will have to do more tests, but it appears to be a tumor."

"Okay," my father said after a moment, clipped and resolute.

"I want you to stay in the hospital for a while. You will probably need surgery."

"Okay."

"And what caused the seizure?" my mother asked. She was so upset that she could not quite put it all together.

"The tumor puts pressure on the brain, which reacts in an abnormal way. The electrical activity of the brain becomes uncontrolled. We'll have to put you on anti-epileptic medication. And corticosteroids to control the swelling of the brain."

"Okay," my father said. This, I thought, was how soldiers are supposed to receive their most difficult orders—no emotion, no questions, only acceptance.

I followed the doctor out into the nurses' station. He picked up a chart and began to scrawl a note.

"What's the prognosis?" I said.

He demurred. "We really can't say. It depends on the type of tumor."

"Please tell me. Ballpark."

He was about to shrug me off, but he sighed and lowered his voice. "It's probably a glioblastoma multiforme. That's bad. We can't be sure yet, but if it is a GBM then the prognosis is very poor. I'm sorry."

I WENT STRAIGHT from the hospital to Anna's new apartment, which was in a ramshackle tenement on the Lower East Side. It was two in the morning by the time I got there, and the neighborhood was deserted, desolate.

"I'm sorry to wake you up," I said when she answered the door. She was wearing a T-shirt and plaid boxer shorts, squinting her eyes into the weak light of the hallway.

"Matt? What's going on?" she said.

"I'll tell you in the morning. I just wanted to stay here tonight."

"Fine, I guess. But you know we can't—" she said, letting a rocking hand-gesture fill in the carnal details.

"That's not why I'm here."

"Why *are* you here?" She was almost able to fully open her eyes, and she regarded me with concern. "What's wrong?"

"I want to be with you. I want this one thing to go right. You and me."

The apartment was meager—a single room with a single window. A broken-down couch and an overturned milk crate defined the living area, next to which sat a rumpled cot. Along one wall were the rudiments of a kitchen. The dining area was a small card table and two folding chairs set by the window. She had hung nothing on the walls.

I fell asleep with her chastely in my arms. When I woke, Anna was up already, sipping tea by the window and basking in the light of the morning sun.

FIVE

THE NEXT DAY, I searched for "glioblastoma multiforme" on the internet and came up with a long list of websites, each one more disturbing than the last. One site, intended for medical students, depicted a brain sliced in half with what appeared at first glance to be the aftereffects of a shotgun injury. The center of the brain was a sodden mess of yellow and red mush that was labeled "GBM." Another site showed pictures of the actual cancer cells, crowded and pink and disorderly. Still other sites yielded downtrending graphs of survival times, updates about new chemotherapeutic drugs, reports of revolutionary treatments available only in Mexico, and a faith healer in Taos, New Mexico, who claimed to specialize in the eradication of glioblastomas and astrocytomas.

I didn't see any point in continuing my education in this manner. Even the name of this disease was horrendous. "Multiforme"—meaning what? That it could take on any form it wished, masquerading as something it was not? That it was so protean as to deserve a special designation for its malignancy?

I clicked back to the search engine and typed a new request: "Imperium Luminis AND cult." The first hit was the website of something called the Imperium Luminis Alert. At the top of the page was a black-and-white photograph of Giuseppe Conti sitting alone in a book-lined room, frowning and staring rather balefully into the camera. The group's mission statement was: "We are dedicated to educating the public about the activities and policies of Imperium Luminis, in the hope that members and their families can make informed decisions about involvement with the group." The e-mail address of the group's director, Gregory Blake, was listed at the bottom of the page. I wrote to him, telling him that I was concerned about a friend who had recently joined Imperium Luminis.

By the next day, Gregory Blake had replied with a long message saying that my concern was justified, and that if I happened to be in the New York area he would be happy to meet with me in person. He suggested Central Park.

I found my way to the hill that he had selected. I sat on a bench, absently watching the progress of joggers and cyclists on the road that encircles the park. For some minutes I tried to anticipate which of the men walking past me could be Gregory Blake. On that uninhibited June morning, sun-drenched and warm, I would not have been disappointed had Blake failed to show—in which case, instead of listening to a forcefully negative evaluation of Imperium Luminis that I knew would upset me, I would continue to lounge on the bench, untroubled by anything other than the periodic and irrepressible recollection of my father's face, white against the white hospital sheets.

A youngish man appeared, pushing a double-wide stroller that bore two sleeping babies. As he approached he slowed and said, "Matthew Kelly?" I stood and shook his hand.

"I'm glad to be able to meet with you," he said. Patting the stroller he said, "Please excuse these guys. I couldn't leave them at home."

I was slightly skeptical about meeting someone I had contacted only through the internet, but the sight of the slumbering babies reassured me; somebody, I thought, even if it was just his wife, had entrusted him with the welfare of these children, so he couldn't be too deranged. Not that he seemed at all crazy—he was a tall man, about thirty, bespectacled and wearing loose-fitting jogging pants and a baseball cap. He looked like any of the other young professionals who haunt the Upper East Side in their exercise clothes and dirty sneakers.

"I've met with dozens of people in your situation," he said, sitting down on the bench beside me. "I know you probably don't feel comfortable revealing all sorts of personal details to someone you just met, so I usually begin by telling the story of what happened to me. My experiences with Imperium Luminis."

His gaze was intense and professional. I sensed that he wanted nothing more in the world than to convince me of what he took to be the truth.

"I grew up in a good Catholic family—Mass every Sunday, parochial schools for the children, the whole nine yards—and when it was time for me to go to college I picked Georgetown, largely because it was run by the Jesuits. My first few months there were pretty awful. First, my high school girlfriend broke up with me, which is not such a tragedy in retrospect but at the time was pretty devastating. Then my father died—very suddenly, of a heart attack. When I returned to campus after the funeral I couldn't do any work. I couldn't do *anything*. I was just paralyzed with loneliness. I stopped going to Mass because clearly God had decided to persecute me for some unknown reason. I was in danger of failing out and I didn't know what to do. I was despondent, totally surrounded by darkness. There seemed to be no point in continuing with anything."

Blake rested his arm on the back of the bench and leaned toward me as he spoke, his voice lowered to a confidential murmur.

"That's when a girl I knew from the dorm, Emily, started hanging out in my room. We did homework together. We ate dinner together. What I needed most of all at that moment was a friend, and I just latched on to her. Losing her would have thrown me back into the depression she had rescued me from."

It was a startling experience to listen to a complete stranger unburdening himself of his most intimate thoughts. He spoke in an earnest tone, pausing every so often to deliberate over the proper word. I wanted to stop him from continuing, simply because I was embarrassed by his openness.

"Emily began to talk about Imperium Luminis. Not until I was dependent on her friendship, you see. I had never heard of Imperium Luminis. At first I thought it was some sort of discussion group for Catholic students. When I met with the priest who ran the Georgetown chapter, he strongly recommended that I recommit myself to God. He said I was losing my faith, that in my depression I was in danger of turning away from the Lord. I wasn't really in the mood for religion, so I tried to keep my distance, which is when Emily began to act strangely. She wouldn't see me anymore. She wouldn't talk to me. When I confronted her she said we couldn't be friends after I had rejected the Light. I went about two weeks without speaking to her. It was unbearable. I had become so dependent on her friendship and love that without her I felt even more alone than before I met her."

I felt sorry for Blake. I realized he was not very different from me in background or temperament. Had things gone somewhat differently, I thought, our roles could have been reversed, with me detailing my unfortunate history to him. His story provoked in me a sense of frustration and dread that was at odds with the flawless summer morning.

"Do you just go around telling your life story to people?" I said.

"I do it because I know how lucky I am. There's an assumption that Imperium Luminis is somehow harmless because they're part of the Catholic Church. But don't underestimate them. These are bad people—not just deluded or foolish, but actively malignant."

"Come on."

"Your friend—Anna, was it? How did she get in touch with you?"

"She showed up one night at my apartment and then started e-mailing me."

"She wanted you to visit her at the Imperium Luminis house. Am I right? She told you she wanted to get back together with you?"

"Yes."

"Don't you see? It's part of their plan. She's recruiting you, the same way Emily recruited me."

I dismissed him with a laugh, although the possibility had already crossed my mind as he told his story. Blake produced a sheaf of paper, from which he read:

"'You must go to the utmost extreme for proselytization. If someone will not willingly enter the Light, then a way must be found to ensure that they do so.' That's Giuseppe Conti on recruitment."

"From *The Pilgrim*?"

"No. That's the public face of Giuseppe Conti—the reformed sinner, the happy servant of God. This is from *The Pandect,* which is only shown to members of Imperium Luminis. These are the rules for how Imperium Luminis actually operates."

One of the babies stirred and began to cry, which woke and incited the other one to tears. Blake lifted them from the stroller and cradled them, one in the crook of each arm. He leaned his face toward them alternately, softly speaking nonsense while jostling them. He asked me to put pacifiers into their mouths. The babies grew quiet after a few minutes of sucking and being soothed. Blake placed them gently into the stroller.

"Where was I?" he said, barely above a whisper. "Emily had done her job. She was supposed to target someone depressed or troubled, someone susceptible to the pitch from Imperium Luminis. And that was me. I would have gone wherever she was. Soon I was attending Mass there, and meeting with the priest and confessing my sins to him in minute detail. When he suggested that I drop a philosophy class, it was the most natural thing in the world to obey him. I felt comfortable there. I had found a solution to my sense of emptiness. I let Imperium Luminis direct me, and it felt good. It felt like freedom."

"How is what you're saying different from any other Catholic group?" I said. "So what if you were confessing to a priest? That's what you're *supposed* to do if you're a Catholic."

"I haven't gotten to the Exercises yet. Do you know about them? Four days in the darkness. That's what they do. They lock you in a room in the total darkness for four days. They give you very little food or water. They grind up benzodiazepine pills and dissolve them in the water to make you more relaxed and receptive to what they tell you. It's all a mind game, an indoctrination. They do research on you before the Exercises. They talk to your friends, your family, the people you grew up with. They go after your weak spot."

"Your weak spot?"

"The object of the Exercises is to destroy you psychologically, to bring you back to square one so that you can be rebuilt as a believer, a member of the Light. *The Pandect* says, 'At the conclusion, the novice should be ashamed of the person he or she was before the Exercises began.' In my case, I had always wanted to be a lawyer. So they tried to take that away from me. They told me that everyone on the Georgetown debate team thought I was a hopeless debater. They suggested I was driven by vanity, or making money, or the acclaim of being on the news. They told me stories about lawyers who got vicious criminals off the hook on technicalities. Conversely, they told me stories about poor, downtrodden people driven to lives of crime and put behind bars by merciless prosecutors."

"And that's all it took? A few stories?"

"It's difficult to describe what happens. They're very persuasive. The whole experience is disorienting. By the end of the four days I was bawling in the dark. I wouldn't have been a lawyer for anything. They kept repeating one phrase over and over: 'True justice comes only from God.' With my life's great ambition suddenly in question, I asked them what I could possibly do. They said it would be revealed to me."

I looked around the park, shocked. I thought of Anna lying in the dark, being worked on by some pernicious interrogator.

"They told Anna she couldn't paint," I said, almost to myself. "She wanted to be an artist."

"And then after the Exercises comes the good stuff. If your family balks at your new life, you're expected to cut off contact with them. That's what I did. My mother, who loved me more than anything, I was convinced was working against me. All your mail and e-mail is monitored by the priest in charge. And have you ever heard of the circlet? It's a barbed bracelet that you wear under your shirt. It draws blood. It's a punishment of the body, mortification of the flesh."

"Punishment for what?"

"For anything. The whole point is to subjugate yourself, to conquer your will. The body is evil, and only obedience to Imperium Luminis can protect you from your base instincts."

I must have been looking at Blake with a strange expression, because he said, "I know. You're wondering why. Why do all this? How could I fall for it? Because it's actually an *accomplishment* to debase yourself this way. It felt wonderful to give control of my life to someone else, especially because I was making such a mess of it on my own. The new plan was that I would get a job, have a family and make some money, most of which I would then turn over to Imperium Luminis. That's the clever thing about them. They don't just leave you in this state of suspended animation. You're sent back out into the world to live an outwardly normal life, but it's like you're a spy. You have a secret life. You are a spy for God. Everyone around you is corrupt, but you know the truth. And then you're told to recruit others, just as you were recruited."

"Holy shit," I said. "This can't be true."

"Doesn't everything I've said fit with what you've seen with Anna?"

I nodded miserably.

"There is a way out, you know. My mother wouldn't accept the loss of her son, and she essentially had me kidnapped. They took me to a hotel in the middle of nowhere and locked me in a room with someone who had left Imperium Luminis. He was able to introduce a seed of doubt into my mind. It wasn't enough at first—I still wanted to be in the Light—but it was a start. I began to think things through a little more clearly. It brought me back to reality. I recognized that the Exercises were manipulative, and I left. Now I'm a lawyer after all. Married with twin daughters."

He glanced at the carriage in a loving way and one of his daughters, who was too young to understand what he was saying, nevertheless smiled and giggled in response to his gaze.

He removed a manila envelope from the undercarriage of the stroller.

"These are some documents and articles you should read, just so you know I'm not making this stuff up. And my number is in there if you need to contact me. I run a business now. I go around talking to members of Imperium Luminis, just as was done for me. The fee is very reasonable."

"I think you should call her stepfather—Carl Barrett."

"*The* Carl Barrett? I can see why Imperium Luminis is so interested in her."

I didn't quite follow him, so he spelled it out: "Money. It's all about money and power."

He stood and grasped the bar of the stroller. As he left he said, offhandedly: "By the way, since you're being recruited by the Light, it's very possible that you're being watched. Any of these joggers may be reporting on this meeting. Just so you're aware."

FROM THE PARK I went directly to the hospital, where my father was providing much diversion for the doctors responsible for his care, or so I guessed by the way their plans for him seemed to change by the hour. In the two days since the seizure he had been placed on a succession of four anti-epileptic medications and a cocktail of steroids. They were going to operate, but an MRI was performed and an expert at Mount Sinai was consulted and finally the determination was made that the tumor was inoperable. They broke the news in exemplary fashion, sober-faced and useless.

I found my father sitting in the hospital chair, swaddled in a cotton blanket, staring out at the blue sky.

"How are you doing?" I said.

"Not so bad. The headache is less today."

We were quiet for several minutes. I wanted to talk about the important issues of our lives, but to do so would mean that we were already beginning to say goodbye. I hewed to small talk and silence, just something to break the monotony of his day, something to distract him from the waiting.

"The Yanks lost yesterday," I said. "Rivera blew the save, if you can believe it."

Normally he would have reacted to this news with animation, with managerial second-guessing—a remark, say, on the need to preserve Rivera's arm for the post-season—but he simply nodded his head. He seemed to be ignoring me.

"What's wrong?" I said.

From underneath his blanket he withdrew his left hand, the hand that was working with reasonable cooperation. He was holding my copy of *The Pilgrim*, which, I now remembered, I had left in his room that first night of his hospitalization.

"I've been reading this," he said. "I'm trying to decide if there's a message in it or not. I'm not sure if Giuseppe Conti is part of it all."

His tone was vague and private, as when someone talks in the midst of sleep.

"Part of what?"

He dropped his voice even further and leaned toward me slightly. "It's been going on this whole time. They've been working to get me for all these years."

"What are you talking about?"

"The enemy. I've seen them again. Moving outside the door."

I stood, gripped by panic and confusion. I tried hurriedly to think of some way that these remarks could be explained or rendered orderly, but I could not.

"I'm going to get your doctor," I said. "You're not yourself."

"They've been asking about you."

"Who has?"

"A priest was here this morning asking all sorts of questions about you."

An improbable thought flashed through my mind.

"Was he from Imperium Luminis?" I said.

It seemed that this possibility had not occurred to him. "Maybe," he said, nodding thoughtfully.

Outside I found the neurologist seated at the nurses' station, copying information from a computer screen into a patient's chart.

"What the hell is wrong with my father?" I said, so loudly and aggressively that the surrounding nurses looked up as well. I lowered my voice. "He's not making any sense."

"I was actually hoping to catch you before you went in," the doctor said. "I'm afraid that the Decadron has produced an abnormal reaction. It's not uncommon in people given such high doses of steroids."

"They've made him lose his mind?"

"It's temporary. We're titrating the dose, and he should be feeling better soon."

I felt a cold and enduring hatred for this doctor, this bow-tied neurologist who was so nonchalant about the catastrophe occurring in my father's brain. Had we been in a bar or a dark street I would have liked to lay into him, to bloody him. Instead I made a note of the occasion for possible use in a malpractice matter.

"He said a priest visited him this morning," I said.

The doctor looked at me quizzically for an instant, before saying, "Oh, he must mean the psychiatrist. I requested a psych consult last night. That's the only other visitor he's had."

"No priests?"

"Not that I know of."

I went back into my father's room. He was holding *The Pilgrim* in his lap.

"Why do you think they left this here for me?" he said.

"*I* left it here, Dad."

"The back cover and the last pages are missing. Is there something significant in the ending that I'm not supposed to see yet?"

"I tore them off because they had blood on them."

But he wasn't listening. He was constructing new arrangements, reassigning meanings. As I listened to him I wondered whether I was hearing the echo of whatever condition it was that had brought him to the VA hospital after the war. Who was the enemy that had been waiting for him all these years? And, more concretely, was this mysterious priest only a phantom, an actual psychiatrist transformed into a pastor by the lens of my father's confusion? Or was everything that Gregory Blake had told me true—and even more?

SIX

HAVING RECLAIMED the copy of *The Pilgrim* from my father, I took it home and threw it on my kitchen table. The next night, as I was finishing a solitary dinner of take-out chicken, I found myself entranced by the artwork on the front cover—that lonely hut, the site of Giuseppe Conti's great revelation, with the bright sky reigning over the darkened landscape. I rummaged through my closet for a battered shoebox that held several years' worth of snapshots. I dug into the layers of pictures until I reached the summer following my first year at Princeton, when Anna had decided to travel to Sicily to spend time with her biological father.

I found the picture I was looking for: Anna, in white shorts and a pink tank top, standing in front of a small stone building on a mountain summit, smiling and poking her head into the doorway in a pose of exaggerated curiosity, playing the moment up for the camera.

The hut looked much the same as in the artist's representation on the book cover.

MAYBE YOU CAN come visit me in Sicily," Anna said one night that spring when the subject of the summer came up.

She seemed to have no idea that more than inertia might prevent me from accompanying her to Sicily. Despite her rejection of Carl Barrett's money, she was not hurting for support; her biological father, Matteo Damiani, was a famous sculptor, and she wanted for nothing at school. I took a mental inventory of my own meager bank account and concluded that I could just about afford the plane fare.

"But I wouldn't be able to pay for anything else over there," I said. "Food, shelter, that kind of thing."

"My father will put you up. Every summer a bunch of art students from all over the world come to study with him. He'll have plenty of room."

That June, just after finals and before I was scheduled to start a summer internship with a law firm in midtown Manhattan, I accompanied Anna to Palermo. I remember the blast of heat as we were disgorged from the back of the small plane onto the shimmering tarmac. In the airport terminal, I heard for the first time Anna speaking Italian. She was fluent, I knew, having been taught in her early childhood by her parents, but it was oddly exciting—even seductive—to hear the ease and grace with which she expressed herself, to watch her waving her hands before her to better punctuate a phrase. She had reverted to her natural state. Italian sounded good and looked even better coming from Anna's lips.

After a slow train ride toward Trapani, during which Anna fell asleep on my shoulder and began to snore audibly, a lurching bus brought us into the interior of the island. We got off in the middle of nowhere, not at a bus stop but a slight dilatation of the shoulder of the road.

"Jennifer will pick us up here," she said.

We were in the midst of vast olive groves that stretched into the distant hills on both sides of the road. The silence of the place was broken only by the occasional bird or lazily buzzing insect.

"Can you believe it was only a few hours ago that we were sitting in McCosh taking exams?" she said. "I've already begun to forget everything."

Soon a small blue dot appeared on the horizon, a car coming in our direction, raising a plume of dust behind itself.

"That's her," Anna said.

Jennifer was Matteo Damiani's second wife. When the car skittered to a stop next to us, I was surprised to find in the driver's seat an attractive blond woman, in her early thirties at the oldest; I knew from photographs that Matteo Damiani was pushing sixty, and I had assumed that Jennifer would be his contemporary. She greeted us warmly and Anna and I climbed into the cramped back seat.

We drove for miles, farther and farther from civilization. All that surrounded us were olive groves and vineyards and increasingly rugged mountains. Every so often we would pass a small abandoned dwelling, but we saw no one. We turned onto a washed-out dirt road that brought us toward the largest structure we had seen since Trapani—a long stone house with several outbuildings, perched on a rise overlooking a vast field. It was an old monastery, now occupied entirely by Damiani and his entourage. Scattered in the nearby field were Damiani's sculptures—undulating metal walls and abstract steel shapes so out of place that they could have dropped from a passing spacecraft.

The interior of the monastery was cool and dark and little renovated; there were electric lights and comfortable furnishings, but the walls and floor remained bare stone, blackened in many places by centuries of candle smoke. Small windows in a central living room admitted shafts of light through the thick, medieval walls.

"Your father's in the studio," Jennifer said. "Go ahead out."

We exited the main building into a cloister that presumably had once held the garden of the resident monks. It was occupied by a small swimming pool, lined with terra-cotta tiles and long tendrils of ivy. The studio was across the cloister, in a smaller building.

We found Matteo Damiani drawing on large sheets of paper with a heavy black marker. When he heard us enter he looked up, scowling, plainly annoyed at having been disturbed. Seeing his daughter, however, he smiled and rushed toward her.

"Anna," he said. "My God, you look so grown up."

He took hold of her face and kissed her forehead vigorously. Only then did he glance my way.

"Welcome," he said, shaking my hand with a crushing grip. He was a large man with a head shaved completely bald. A sharp nose and glinting eyes gave him the aspect of a bird of prey. He produced large-scale metal sculptures and installations, and his build and demeanor were more suggestive of a construction foreman than an effete artist.

He and Anna exchanged a few words in Italian; the gist of it seemed to concern my identity. He asked a question—perhaps, was I her boyfriend?—to which Anna nodded. Damiani asked me, "How long will you be with us?"

"Only a week. I have to get back home to start a job."

"I hope you're planning to work with us on the pieces while you're here."

I nodded. His accent was strong and he spoke in a low voice, so that I had to puzzle out his words.

"We are one big family around here," he said, putting his large arm around my shoulders. "People come to live here, work with me, maybe learn a little, but most of all to have a good time, to enjoy life for a while. I'd like to think there's no more beautiful spot in the entire world."

He gazed out the doorway at the cloister and the venerable stone walls, at the fields stretching toward the mountains in the distance.

"As for the question of sleeping arrangements—" he said. Anna and I looked at each other sheepishly. Damiani grunted and regarded me as if aware of the carnal nature of my most secret thoughts about his daughter. Then, abruptly, he began to laugh.

"I'm only kidding," he said. "Our philosophy here is *va bene*—just do what makes you happy. You two will be staying in a room in the main building. Jennifer will show you where."

And with that, he picked up his marker and returned to his frenetic sketching.

THERE WERE TEN students in residence, in addition to Anna and me. We were introduced to them all, but it took me several days to put names with faces. They were from Germany and France and the United States and Japan and Brazil, all engaged for the summer to live with and learn from the master. One was writing her doctoral dissertation on Damiani. Most were our age, but two or three looked to be in their forties. Matteo and Jennifer presided over the scene, the leaders of a lively and bohemian community.

That first night we shared a group dinner of fresh pasta and tomatoes from a garden on the hillside. There were olives from the nearby fields, and wine made in the basement from the local grapes. It was sweet and pungent and cool, and it tasted of the earth. We lingered over the table as an evening breeze came through the windows, agitating the candlelight. Long after the food was gone, the pitchers of wine kept coming. I was becoming a little drunk, feeling a welcome lightness in my legs and a pleasant dulling of my thoughts. The rest of the group was in a similar state— laughing uproariously and contagiously at comments that would not have been funny to someone in a normal frame of mind.

Anna was a little more affected by the wine than the others were. She put her hand on my leg and leaned against my shoulder, which I thought was potentially too bold in the presence of her father. But neither Damiani nor the others took notice—perhaps, in Damiani's case, because he had downed two glasses for every one that the rest of us drank.

"How is your mother?" Damiani said to Anna.

She sat up and searched for the correct word. She found it and said, in an icy voice, *"Troubled."*

The boisterous mood at the table turned somber. People looked down at their empty plates.

"She's totally concerned with her status in New York," Anna said. "She has a full-time publicist now. She doesn't actually *do* anything worth publicizing, of course, other than spending money. She used to be so different."

"Maybe not so different," Damiani said. "Why do you think she married me? An up-and-coming artist heading off to New York, making lots of money, being celebrated at galleries all over the city."

"Believe me, things have changed. Everything about her is stifling now."

"And Carl?"

"Strange as ever. Moody, arrogant. A bastard."

Why, I wondered, were they having this discussion surrounded by near-strangers? I realized that we were not, in fact, strangers. In Damiani's mind we were disciples, and so unquestionable was his greatness that he had no need to hide any matter from us. Anna, for her part, was willing to bad-mouth her mother and stepfather to anyone, even sober.

Anna and I took a postprandial walk in one of the olive groves. The sky was a faint, lingering blue, but everything below the treeline was in shadows.

"How exactly did your father end up here?" I said.

"The divorce was about six years ago. We all used to be very happy. My father was a pretty gallant figure, you know, and my mother liked being squired around by a famous artist. Then everything changed. He came down with this strange disease that has a name I can never remember. Gillian Barry or something. He was paralyzed. He was in Saint Vincent's for a month on a respirator. When he got out, he wouldn't stop talking about how much he wanted to move back to Sicily, back to where he and my mother had grown up. I guess his sickness made him think about his priorities, and he realized that work was more important than parties. Sicily was more peaceful and fulfilling than New York. My mother said absolutely not, and things got worse from there."

"They couldn't have moved here part-time?"

"I think Sicily wasn't the real issue. They just made it the issue instead of talking about everything else. I mean, my father married Jennifer only two months after the divorce. Was he seeing her beforehand? I don't know. There are some things I just don't want to know."

I thought of my own folks, my boring, uncomplicated parents who would not have divorced under any circumstances. If my father had turned out to be a serial killer, if my mother were unmasked as a spy for the Russians, I believe they would have simply soldiered on. The matters that Anna discussed in such a commonplace tone would have been incomprehensible to them. A famous artist having a near-death experience and decamping to rural Italy. An abandoned wife taking up with a real-estate mogul and becoming a fixture in the tabloid gossip columns. The thought occurred to me that what truly separated my family from Anna's was a discrepancy not in money or breeding, but simply in affinity for the exotic.

"So your mother came from around here?" I said.

"Right down that road. She was as provincial as provincial can be. So was my father. They fell in love and went to New York and it turned out that everybody loved his sculptures. The rest is history."

"When I first met your mother I thought she was some sort of Italian heiress."

Anna lowered her voice, even though we were in the middle of the deserted countryside and it was impossible that anyone else could be listening.

"Can you keep a secret?" she said. "Carl Barrett isn't exactly who he presents himself as, either. He grew up dirt poor in Brooklyn."

"So wait a minute—why are they so anxious about *my* background?"

She shrugged and laughed. "Because they're assholes."

On our way back to the monastery we passed the swimming pool in the cloister. Anna grabbed my hand and said, with a mischievous grin, "Let's go for a swim."

Before I could say anything, she was taking off her clothes. She meant to go in naked.

"Hold on," I said, scandalized.

"Who cares? Look at where we are."

She had already thrown her shirt to the ground, and my first impulse was to pick it up in the name of decency and hold it across her naked, exquisite body. I glanced around to make sure no one was looking. Maybe it was the lingering effects of the wine, but for some reason in that idyllic setting—just past dusk, with the light fading and the sweet fragrance of the nocturnal flowers beginning to intensify—I realized that there was absolutely nothing to hide. I stripped and took her hand and, together, we dove in.

I made two phone calls the next day. The first was to Alitalia. I asked about switching my return ticket to the end of August. The ticket agent clicked away on a keyboard, made the substitution and charged me thirty dollars. The next call was to my father.

"What are you talking about?" he said. "You have a job in New York."

"I also have a job here."

"Doing what?"

"Working with Anna's father on his sculptures."

Silence.

"You're old enough that I can't tell you what to do, so I won't. But try to show a little responsibility. In the real world, people have jobs and they stick with them. When you apply to law school, do you think they'll be more impressed with an internship at Sloan, Ames and Quigley or a summer sunning yourself in Italy?"

I T W A S N O T until the middle of the summer that Anna suggested we visit the hut where Giuseppe Conti received his vision of Imperium Luminis. At the time, I considered it a good excuse for a trip through the countryside, the purpose picked almost at random. Only later would the whole thing take on an aura of predestination.

The Damiani compound possessed three cars, none of which had automatic transmissions, and none of which, therefore, I was able to operate. This was a source of great amusement to the European members of the household, no matter how many times I told them that manual transmissions were as common in New York City as the burros that grazed in the fields below the compound. Anna had learned to drive a stick in previous summers in Sicily, so for our road trip she was in control of the wheel. The significance of this was that she thought certain laws of physics did not apply to whatever sector of the earth happened to hold her vehicle. Two cars traveling in opposite directions could surely occupy the same space at the same time; otherwise, how to explain the abandon with which she passed slower cars on blind, hairpin curves? Anna was genetically Sicilian, she had learned to drive in Sicily, and nature and nurture had combined to produce a truly dangerous specimen. In one small town, she nearly sideswiped a car and got into a heated, hand-waving dispute with the other driver over who was at fault. She was so agitated that her Italian failed her and she lapsed into English, at which her adversary raised his hands and rolled his eyes in theatrical incomprehension.

We kept the radio on as we drove eastward toward the Madonie mountains. Anna would sing along and sometimes translate the words. Either she was having fun with me, or Italian pop songs have the filthiest lyrics I have ever heard.

"I want you to take off your clothes and rub yourself," she would say, half singing.

"You're kidding."

"This is the night we come seventeen times."

"*Anna*."

"It's a loose translation, okay?"

I admired the view of Anna as much as I did the panorama of the rising mountains. The wind through the window lashed her long dark hair. She wore delicate sunglasses and a sleeveless pink top that revealed the freckles on her bronze shoulders.

We became stuck behind a slow-moving farm truck. Anna worked the gearshift and swung into the oncoming lane without an adequate view of the road ahead. All at once a black Mercedes was bearing down on us, blaring its horn, only a few milliseconds from hitting us head-on. I shouted some primitive noise of terror and Anna downshifted and pulled back in behind the truck.

"These roads are getting way too crowded," she said, pretending to be nonchalant but, for once, disconcerted by her own driving.

We were thankfully within a few miles of the isolated trailhead, where we parked and got out of the car. I was relieved to have reached the place physically intact. The escarpments and limestone peaks of the Madonie range loomed above us.

"Are you sure this is doable?" I said, staring at the trail, which began its ascent at an angle of about sixty degrees.

Anna quoted from our Laughing Planet guidebook. "'The well-marked trail to the Conti hut is challenging but not dangerous. Allow six hours for the round trip, and bring plenty of water and protection from the sun. The perseverant will be rewarded with an extraordinary view and a pleasant picnic locale.'"

The guidebook, as it turned out, was overly optimistic. The hike was extremely difficult, the sun fierce and unrelenting. We went straight uphill for more than an hour before stopping to reassess the situation. Anna sat on the ground and took a greedy swig from our water bottle. I bent over to catch my breath. Sweat ran in rivulets down my face and dripped onto the parched ground, where it evaporated immediately.

"Let's turn around," I said. "This is ridiculous."

She looked at me defiantly. "No way. Not after we've come this far."

"Why do you want to see this stupid hut so badly?"

"I did a lot of reading about Imperium Luminis for the Slagle class. I just want to see where it all began."

"This better be pretty spectacular," I said, gazing up at the remainder of the ascent, beginning to regret my decision to research Justin the Gnostic—although surely, even in the absence of Slagle's list of topics, some principle of universal necessity or equilibrium would have compelled Anna to find that mountain, located as it was on the small island of her parents' birth. Her excitement grew in proportion to our altitude, as though even then she could guess at the significance that the destination would hold for her in the future.

After two more hours of hard climbing, we reached a level plateau, a kind of saddle between two larger massifs. In the distance was the touristy coastal town of Cefalú, its flamingo-pink hotels flanking a sea that faded indistinctly into the blue horizon. Before us stood a tiny stone hut, perhaps ten feet square, covered with a wooden roof.

"Finally," I said.

We walked around the exterior, looking the walls up and down. I snapped the picture of Anna poking her head into the doorway.

"They take care of it," Anna said. "The roof is new."

"Who takes care of it?"

"Imperium Luminis."

"Shouldn't there be a sign or something? I'm surprised they don't make this into a big tourist destination. Think of all the people who go to Assisi and Lourdes."

"That's totally against the Imperium Luminis philosophy. They're a very private group. The last thing they would want is to have all sorts of tourists crawling over their shrine."

Once inside, it took a moment for our eyes to adjust to the darkness. We found a wooden cot, a desk and a chair.

"This is where Giuseppe Conti wrote *The Pilgrim,*" Anna said, running her hand over the desk. I was surprised by her reverent tone. "And here is where he had his dream."

I sat on the bed and stretched out. I put my index fingers to my temples.

"Wait, wait—I'm having a vision," I said.

"Very funny." She looked out the small window toward the sea. "Wouldn't it be wonderful, though, to have a vision? To have that purpose, that certainty? Giuseppe Conti walked out of this hut convinced that he had seen the face of God. And you know what? Even if he was wrong, I think he was lucky."

I will never forget her expression. The face I knew and all that went along with it—her confidence, her self-assurance, her blithe contentment—had been displaced by some deeper strain of anxiety and longing. She looked almost heartbroken. I didn't know what to say. She turned to me.

"What are we doing here?" she said—meaning in the broadest sense.

I wanted to stop her from continuing in this vein, because I could answer this question no better than she could. I responded in the only way I knew how. I stood behind her, my arms around her waist, kissing her neck on the soft spot just below her ear.

"I love you," I said, at which she sighed and nodded and looked up toward the ceiling.

"—Look at that!" she said with a sharp intake of breath, breaking away from me.

I followed her eyes toward the ceiling. From the alarm in her voice, I expected to see either a dangerous animal or a sign from God. Instead, it was a video camera, well hidden, nestled in the corner where the wall met the roof. It was trained directly on us.

"Do you think anyone is watching?" she said.

The lens was a dull, lifeless gray.

"Let's get out of here," I said.

As we left the hut Anna looked back at the camera and said, shaking her head, "That is *so* Imperium Luminis."

THAT SUMMER WAS a freedom of the sort I doubt I will ever experience again. When I returned home, my father picked me up at the airport. He said nothing for the first few minutes of the drive home. Then, as if he had been waiting to say the words all summer long, he burst out: "Just tell me one thing. What are you doing with your life? How are you going to get into law school if you go gallivanting around like this? Opportunities are passing you by."

"Let them pass."

This related to his grand plan for me, not my own, and I felt no guilt in contradicting it.

"It's important for you to get ahead," he said.

"What about you? What have you done with *your* life that's so great? Why am *I* the one who has to do all these big things? Can't I just be happy for a few months?"

He didn't answer for several miles. Finally he said, "I have made sacrifices for you."

"What sacrifices? You mean the tuition money?"

He sighed—a melodramatic, long-suffering sigh, I thought at the time—and turned on the radio, finding the Yankees game.

Had I known at that time something more of his complicated past, I certainly would not have been so blunt, so petulant. And yet I still believe that my larger point was legitimate. When I think back on my time in college—in fact, when I think back on my entire life—those memories of Sicily are among my best. Driving along the Mediterranean coast in a fast car with a beautiful girl who loves you, zipping in and out of long tunnels, gazing upon an infinity of blue water, all while singing along with pop songs in demotic Italian—if that, or something very much like it, is not what we are put on earth for, then I truly know nothing.

SEVEN

TAKEN TOGETHER, the documents from Gregory Blake painted a portrait of an organization that operated on a grand scale. Imperium Luminis was a multinational conglomerate with activities in every corner of the world, each branch toiling for a goal that could be seen entirely and comprehended fully only at the highest levels. (Of course, as one of the articles pointed out, members of Imperium Luminis believed that this higher level of direction constituted God Himself.) Much was made of the fact that several of the Pope's closest advisers were in Imperium Luminis. The implication was that, because of the Pope's numerous infirmities, these advisers were actually running the

Church. There were reports of vast amounts of cash pouring into the coffers of the Vatican, all from the contributions of devoted members of Imperium Luminis. The articles claimed that Imperium Luminis recruited especially from the ranks of the highest achievers and the most powerful families, as these were the people predisposed to acquire influence in the outside world. Members were said to secretly number among the most prominent politicians, judges, bankers, businessmen and editors—an army of agents working silently for God and, perhaps, awaiting the appearance of a coming signal.

I replaced the articles in their envelope. I was sitting in a dismal Chinese takeout across the street from Anna's building, munching on an egg roll and watching the window. From my vantage I could see her doorway, but I was concealed behind a garbage can, placed so that when she emerged onto the street she would be unlikely to see me. In the window, a string of multicolored Christmas lights blinked in a hectic and indecipherable pattern, although it was June and, especially in the greasy steam of the little restaurant, oppressively hot. A sizable cockroach raced across the floor, a blur of legs and probing antennae. I put down my egg roll and debated whether or not to swallow what was already in my mouth.

It had been five days since I had gone over to Anna's apartment from my father's bedside. I had expected that, thus reunited, we would be able to spend a great deal of time together. But Anna was keeping largely to herself, working all day at her menial job in midtown and then visiting the Imperium Luminis house in the evenings.

"I'll have more free time in a few weeks," she told me. "After that we'll be able to hang out all we want."

Twice I called her late at night and she didn't even answer the phone. So, increasingly suspicious of the Light and hoping to discover whatever

Anna was concealing, I had set myself up in the squalid noodle shop across from her building.

I almost missed her when she appeared, breezing out the doorway and moving quickly downtown. I grabbed my bag and sprinted out into the dark street, tossing the remainder of the egg roll into the trash. Anna was already a block away, toting a large backpack stuffed almost to capacity. I settled into a pursuit that would maintain that distance of separation. She was wearing light khaki pants and a white shirt, which made it easy to keep sight of her, a white figure marching through the dim precincts of the Lower East Side.

Her destination was a small concrete playground near the East River. A swing set sat unused behind a chain-link fence. The basketball court was missing a hoop on one end. Stray scraps of paper and trash littered the ground. On the concrete embankment that surrounded the place, amidst the general graffiti of names and painted-over tags, someone had scrawled the words, TO WHOM IT MAY CONCERN, followed by a series of obscenities.

Two men were sitting on a bench at the far end of the playground, beyond which the FDR Drive whispered and groaned with its traffic. Anna approached them. I was too far away to hear the conversation. The men shook their heads in response to her questions. The only explanation I could arrive at for this scene was that Anna was there to buy drugs. After a few more words were exchanged, Anna handed something to one of the men and walked toward the far gate of the playground.

When she was almost out of sight, I approached the men. They eyed me warily as I drew closer.

"I was hoping you could help me out," I said, too formally. "What did that girl just say to you?"

They glanced at each other and seemed to confer silently over who I was and what was to be done about me. They looked ragged and glassy-eyed, but not dangerous. I took out a ten from my wallet and gave it to one of them.

"Hey now, this is an equal partnership," the other said. I gave him some money as well.

"She was talking to us about God and redemption," the first one said. "We just come out here to enjoy the night. You know what I'm saying? People will talk to you about the craziest shit."

"She wasn't looking to buy drugs?"

"What are you? A cop?"

I turned and sprinted in the direction that Anna had gone. I caught sight of her again just as she was disappearing down a set of subway stairs. I bounded down the stairs and almost ran into her around the first corner. She had paused to talk to a homeless woman who was sprawled across the stairway landing. I retreated behind the wall.

"Do you have anyplace to go tonight?" Anna said.

"If I did, do you think I would be here?"

Anna gave the woman a slip of paper.

"This is the name of a shelter. It's safe and clean and you can have your own private room."

"What's the catch? Who are you, anyway?"

Anna removed a small brown paper bag from her backpack and handed it to the woman, who took it skeptically, as if it might be rigged to explode.

"God has not forgotten you," Anna said, and moved on.

I stood behind the corner and watched as the woman carefully opened the bag. She took out a substantial sandwich and a can of soda and, without a moment's pause, began to devour the food.

This went on for two hours. Anna rode the subways at random, look-ing for the lonely, the addicted, the desperate. I stayed in the car be-hind her, pulled my baseball cap over my eyes, hid behind columns and stairways. I was struck by how beautiful she was, how angelic she must have appeared to these people—a young woman dressed in white, her long hair falling in ropy curls, speaking to them of safety and God. It occurred to me that her white outfit might have been chosen specifi-cally to produce this impression. Was she really just providing these people with assistance, or was this a way to attract new recruits to the Light?

The crowd thinned as the hour grew later. Anna was undeterred by the increasingly lonely passageways and deserted stations. Would she keep this up all night? Finally, on a platform somewhere beneath deep Brooklyn, she engaged a man in conversation. I could not hear their words. When the encounter began Anna was standing and the man was sitting on a bench. He rose and stood quite close to her. Anna stepped away, turning her back to the wall. The man was fingering something in his pocket.

"Hey—Anna!" I said loudly, coming out from behind a pole and walk-ing down the platform. "Anna! What a coincidence!"

I eyed the man to see what he would do. I was unarmed, of course, but among the things I inherited from my father were his height and an intermittent glint in the eye that made him look, in my mother's words, like "a goddamned crazy Irishman."

Anna looked at me in shock and, I'm quite certain, with relief. The man backed away and retreated down the platform.

"What are you doing here?" she said. "You've been following me?"

"Let's go back to your place, okay? Enough of this nonsense."

DURING THE TRIP back to Anna's apartment we were sullen and silent. I was angry with her for wandering around in the dangerous corners of the night asking for trouble; she was annoyed with me for reasons I could not comprehend. I had, after all, just delivered her from what was at least an awkward encounter and possibly a prelude to physical harm. We watched the passing stations, avoiding each other's eyes. Whatever we were going to say would be said back in the apartment. In the meantime, I occupied myself with constructing an argument so logical that she could not fail to see the imperfections of her new life.

We walked quickly to her building through the deserted streets. The neighborhood, which was questionable even in the daylight, became ominous at night. I had the sense that people or things were watching from the shadows, waiting for us to pass. In the far distance a single police siren wailed. Anna jingled the keys in the lock and we ascended the dark staircase of the old tenement building, the kind that my ancestors—or hers, depending on the vagaries of immigration from Sicily— might have known, smelling of generations of boiled cabbage and meat.

She threw her bag on the floor once we were in the apartment. I registered anew the smallness of the place, the dim shadows, the borderline squalor—the dirty window, the hand-me-down couch, the milk-crate seats. We sat at her rickety table, taking up positions across from each other.

"What were you doing out there?" she said, her eyes flashing with anger.

"What was *I* doing? What were *you* doing out there?"

"Bringing the Light to people who need it."

"What you were doing was dangerous."

She looked at me defiantly. "I was in God's hands."

"That last guy was going to hurt you. I know you know it, too. He was holding something in his pocket and backing you into the corner. What would have happened if I hadn't been there?"

She shrugged.

"Let me get this straight," I said. "In order to deliver a few sandwiches and chat up some junkies and lunatics about God, you're willing to risk your life. How does this make any sense?"

"It makes perfect sense. My life is worth nothing. The Light is everything."

"Don't you realize how crazy this is?"

"Maybe from the perspective of someone who lives only for this world. You remember the prayers, don't you? 'Let us build the City of God.'"

I would love to be able to report that her tone was wild and strident, that her demeanor revealed some fundamental imbalance or disconnection from reality—it would have been much easier to dismiss her words if that were the case. But she was calm and reserved. She continued, leaning toward me:

"Either you believe or you don't. There is no middle ground. If you do believe, then this is what you do. You put yourself totally in God's hands, give yourself completely to a vision of a better world. How can I say I believe and then turn around and say I'm too scared to bring comfort to those who need it? How can I say I believe, but only just so much that I don't have to change the way I am? Everything has to change. Everything."

"If everything changes, then our relationship changes, too. Is that what you want?"

"What I really want is for you to see how wonderful Imperium Luminis is. Keep an open mind. Don't be so threatened."

"I look around here and all I see is what Imperium Luminis has taken away from you. Why live in a place like this?"

"What more do I need?"

"How about a place that isn't infested with roaches? A place that doesn't have rat traps in the foyer?"

She was silent for a moment. "You don't understand. This is just temporary, an optional follow-up phase to the Exercises. All of this is like an illusion."

I banged my hand on the table, which startled her.

"See? This is real," I said. "This is not an illusion. Or am I an illusion, too? You're fucking up your life because you can't separate what's real from what's an illusion."

"Meaning that the Light is the illusion?"

I removed the manila envelope full of articles from my bag and began to page through them.

"I want you to read some of these articles."

"Let me guess. Gregory Blake."

I looked up in surprise, remembering Blake's warning that we were being watched during our meeting. Was it possible that someone had observed us and discussed the matter with Anna?

"He's a one-man crusade, that guy," she said. "What is it again? 'The Imperium Luminis Alert'? Don't believe a word of what he says. He's just consumed by hatred. He'll say anything to make the Light look bad."

I pushed an article across the table to her.

"*Time* magazine," I said, reading the headline: "'Charismatic Catholic Leader Spent Time as Psychiatric Patient.'"

"I've read that one already," she said. "The Benefactor had to hide from his former Mafia associates after his conversion, so he checked himself into a Catholic hospital under an assumed identity."

She looked at me complacently, awaiting my next objection.

"But it says he had paranoid ideas, that he believed he was the Son of God."

"Well they had to put something down in the hospital records, didn't they?"

I tried with another article, from *The New Yorker*.

"I've seen that one, too," she said. "It's all about the powerful politicians and media figures who are secretly members of Imperium Luminis, right? That's so obviously an anti-Catholic stereotype, like saying Jews are cheap or whatever is anti-Semitic. Catholics are the big bad papists secretly conspiring to take over the world, or at least America? Please."

"So you deny that this article is reporting facts?"

"I deny its conclusion. Look, even if I grant your argument that some influential people belong, how is that illogical? If the mission of the Light is to sanctify the world, what better way to make a difference than to work with people in power?"

This was going poorly. I had imagined, on the subway coming back from Brooklyn, that Anna would receive these articles with something like wide-eyed shock and dismay, that my words alone would be enough to change her mind—which was instead, in characteristic fashion, stubbornly resistant to movement. I decided to stop pushing articles at her, since she had apparently been briefed in advance about every possible charge against Imperium Luminis.

"The issue isn't so much what you believe as how you came to believe it," I said. "That's what really bothers me."

"And what do you think happened?"

"They locked you in a dark room, forced you to fast and gave you some kind of drugs. They interrogated you and went after your psychological weak spot."

Anna burst out laughing.

"I'm sorry," she said. "But that's just such a caricature. The Exercises are a beautiful, contemplative process. Hundreds of thousands of people have done them."

"Am I wrong about what goes on?"

"Well, the dark room is true. And there is fasting. The thing about drugs is a lie. It's actually very similar to psychoanalysis. You devote yourself to learning who you are and why you behave in a given way. 'There is no peace but through reflection and self-discipline.'"

"But they push you toward a certain answer. They manipulate you."

"It's really not like that. I think the only way to convince you of how silly you're being is for you to do the Exercises yourself."

How I wish she had not said that. I was willing to entertain the possibility that Anna was in the right on many of the issues we had been discussing, but when she began to suggest that I would be happier as a member of Imperium Luminis, I could not help but recall the story of Gregory Blake and how his girlfriend had recruited him. I wouldn't have believed Anna capable of it, and I tried to maintain my disbelief, but she continued:

"I want you to be a part of my life," she said. "I want you to understand the Light."

"No way."

"You can undertake the Exercises without becoming a member, you know."

"I said no."

I had started the conversation with what I thought would be incontrovertible proof of the shortcomings of Imperium Luminis, but somehow I had ended up on the defensive, with Anna seeking to change *my* life rather than vice versa.

"You still believe in God, don't you?" she said.

"Not really."

"That's what I would have said before I found Imperium Luminis. Have you been reading *The Pilgrim*?"

I remembered, in a sort of reverie, Anna as she was at Princeton. At dinner, smoking a cigarette, flecks of yellow and red oil paint decorating her arms. Me with a tray of food, approaching. Anna turning and saying, "Hey hon," then throwing her head back for a kiss. She was so beautiful, so cool, so perfectly mine. Or, in a memory of similar vintage, Anna painting in the mornings in Sicily, meditatively mixing colors and spreading them across her canvas, totally contented and consumed by the work. "The light in the morning is perfect for painting," she told me. "In the afternoon everything is too washed-out. The sun is too intense." I had no idea of such things.

I looked across the small card table in her apartment. Anna was regarding me with large, innocent eyes, her hair pulled back into a tight bun. I could hardly make any connection between the carefree, vibrant person I used to love and this earnest creature of God. I could trace the trajectory that she had followed, I could hear the echoes of her old self in her phrasing and voice, but I understood for the first time that she had changed in a truly fundamental way. I could either keep trying to make out the old within the new—keep trying to rebuild our lost world in its original configuration—or I could give up. At that moment the lateness of the hour caught up with me and I was overcome by an exhaustion that felt like sickness.

"I can't be with you this way," I said, almost before I had decided to say it.

I stood to leave. It seemed wrong to simply walk out the door, so I went around the card table and put my hand on her forehead. "Goodbye," I said, allowing the word to bear the weight of an entire mono-logue. I did not necessarily mean to suggest that I would never see her again, although at that moment I couldn't imagine what further visits would accomplish beyond a reiteration of the discussion we had just completed. I leaned over to kiss her, fully expecting that she would turn her cheek to me, rejecting anything remotely sexual as a sin before God. Instead, she turned her chin up and caught my lips with hers. We stayed that way for a long moment.

When I broke away she stood, sliding her body against mine, her sur-prising intention clear though unspoken.

"Wait," I said. "Are you sure this is what you want?" Against the urg-ings of desperate instinct, I was prepared to remind her of her obliga-tions. She answered me by putting her hands behind by head and kissing me. She did not have to say anything. It had been two years since we had been together—too long, too many obstacles, too many complications. Touching her felt so right, so long overdue that it seemed impossible that anyone, even Imperium Luminis, could find grounds to object.

In the course of the night, while running my hand over Anna's bare arm, I felt a tiny sticker of some sort. There were more of these stickers encircling her upper arm. I explored further and realized that they were not stickers at all, but tiny scabs. It was the mark left by the circlet, the barbed bracelet that Gregory Blake had told me about. Had I discovered the scabs under different circumstances I would have been furious and repulsed, more certain than ever that Imperium Luminis was hurting Anna. But since she was at that moment astride my lap, kissing me with undistractable focus and allowing her hair to spill over my head and the surrounding pillow, I did not let the scabs bother me. After all, Anna had faced a choice—either follow the rules of Imperium Luminis or sleep with me—and she had chosen the path of sin, which was, to me at least, a sign of her redemption. I had won her away from Imperium Luminis.

When the sun came up we were both lying in bed.

"How do you feel about this?" she said.

I nuzzled into her hair. "Are you kidding? That was unbelievable."

She turned away.

"What's the matter?" I said.

"I don't know. I don't know anything."

I DIDN'T HEAR from Anna for several days. As the silence lengthened I grew increasingly worried. She wouldn't even pick up the phone.

I went over to her place and knocked on the door. There was no answer—and neither sound nor sign of life from inside. I went back three days in a row before finally becoming concerned for her safety.

"Moved out last week," the super said when I tracked him down. "Just up and left. Rent paid in full through the month, though. What, your girlfriend?"

I insisted that he show me the room. Sure enough, it was empty. The finality and speed of her disappearance stunned me. As I looked around the bare room it seemed that she had never even been there, that her brief reintroduction to my life had been a dream. I had been wrong about winning her back. Given a chance to make our relationship right, to push for a happiness that even then I believed was still possible to achieve, I had been defeated by the Light.

EIGHT

WHEN THE TRANSATLANTIC Building was constructed in the mid-1980s, architecture critics lamented the design in the strongest possible terms, calling it "vulgar" and "a monstrosity" and "a warty excrescence on the Manhattan skyline." The building rises above the surrounding edifices, a slab of gray glass stretching higher and higher until the mind of the viewer begins to question the veracity of the eye's perspective, finally topping out at seventy-one stories, at which point a series of clear, triangular pinnacles continues the ascent toward the heavens. The triangles are changeable in aspect, and I have always believed that this accounts for the esteem in which New Yorkers came to hold the building, despite the initial condemnation of the critics. On some days, the triangles are translucent, almost indistinguishable from the greater sky. At other times, water cascades down their surfaces, producing the incongruous sight of a waterfall atop one of the tallest buildings in midtown. Other days reveal an opaque cloud of smoke filling the triangles. At night they are illuminated in colors that change very slowly. One can look at the building and observe, say, deep red and ochre, and glance again an hour later to discover jazzy pink and blue, the transformation so gradual that constant observation will reveal no discrete change. People who see the building every day swear that it has moods, bad days and good days, periods of silent joy and inexplicable despondency that mirror the goings-on of the surrounding city.

As a child, I watched the building going up. From the second floor of my family's house in Astoria, just across the East River from Manhattan, I could see the steel skeleton being hoisted into place by giant praying-mantis cranes, followed by the glass skin, and finally by the unexpected triangles. I loved the building from the start. It expressed something that I felt was lacking in my life. On our side of the river the houses were drab and the streets were filled with moribund factories, but just across the channel something extraordinary was happening. Someone (I could hardly imagine who) had had a grand vision and was bringing into being an object that embodied the grandeur and grace that I longed for.

When I met Anna in high school I didn't immediately realize that she was the stepdaughter of the man who put up the Transatlantic Building. Even after I learned that her stepfather was a real-estate developer, it was still some time before I made the connection. I can honestly say that the first stirrings of my desire for Anna had nothing to do with her family affiliation. When I gazed out at the incipient Transatlantic Building I had no inkling that my history would involve the originator of that brash gift to the city, or that my story would come to reflect certain elements of the building itself—the remote beauty, the sublime indifference, the changeable light.

From street level I could barely glimpse the illuminated triangles, directly under which Carl Barrett kept his offices. The light from the triangles shot into the dark, misty sky as crisply as the beam from a lighthouse. I pushed through a large revolving door and into the lobby, which was outfitted entirely with Carrara marble and accented with gold. A security guard asked my destination and instructed me to press my thumb onto a small glass screen. A green glow, as from a photocopier, illuminated the screen and my fingerprint appeared on an adjacent computer monitor.

The elevator shuddered as it rose into the sky, fast enough that I felt the acceleration, a heaviness in the gut. I yawned to release the pressure in my ears several times before I reached the seventieth floor, where I found a receptionist sitting beneath a large sign: BARRETT PROPERTIES, stretching across the wall in gold letters.

"I'm here to see Mr. Barrett," I said. "He's expecting me."

Without a word, she escorted me to the inner sanctum through twists and turns of cubicles and hallways. It was eight o'clock in the evening and the place was deserted. The overhead lights had been dimmed, casting shadows over the labyrinth of desks, the slumbering computers, the abandoned paperwork. We reached a small, richly appointed seating area with a view over the East River and Queens.

"Have a seat," she said. "He'll be with you shortly."

I sank into the plush couch and tried to suppress a growing unease. I never looked forward to seeing Carl Barrett. My association with him had begun on an unpleasant note. Soon after I met Anna in high school, I invited her out to Astoria to see a movie with me. We had a great time together and even stole a few minutes in my basement to kiss inexpertly.

When it was time for her to leave, she summoned her stepfather's driver, who appeared in front of our house in a black Mercedes. I was watching from the front window as Carl Barrett himself emerged from the back seat and looked around. I will never forget the expression on his face—a shifting gaze from side to side, a bemused smile, as if he could not understand how Anna had ended up in such a run-down neighborhood. The street that day was covered with soot from a nearby incinerator, which periodically sent an acrid smoke and a fine coat of Dickensian ash over the houses and cars and people and dogs of Astoria. I heard his words to his stepdaughter as she approached the car: "So is *this* garden spot where you want to live when you grow up?" He bundled her into the car, and soon thereafter came an ultimatum from him and his wife: as long as Anna was living under their roof, she was not to associate with the likes of me.

I had often wondered that breeding and class could have been so prominent in Carl Barrett's mind as to have prevented him, sight unseen, from giving a chance to a working-class Irish kid. When Anna revealed the secret of his past—that he himself was born penniless—I was outraged. Who was he to question me and my legitimacy when *he* was only a few steps removed from a similar position? But as I thought about the matter I realized that it actually made perfect sense, in a perverse way, that someone new to the upper class would be hypersensitive to the nuances of behavior, to the subtle messages that would suggest he didn't really belong. Since Anna had sworn me to secrecy, I never yielded to the temptation to call him a hypocrite, to throw his history in his face.

Despite Anna's initial rejection at Princeton of the Barrett name and money, Carl Barrett and Anna's mother had remained stubbornly a part of her life. The three of them reminded me of a family of porcupines, continually frustrated in their attempts at closeness by their natural defenses. Their every interaction was exhausting, fraught with hidden meanings and arcane allusions to arguments of the past. Whenever I spent time during those years with Carl Barrett and his wife, they tolerated me—in their prickly way—with obvious displeasure.

"He has some news to discuss with you," his secretary had told me over the phone. "Come by the office tonight around eight." I had swallowed my pride, put on my best shirt and arrived at the appointed time. The news had to be about Anna.

I stood and walked to the window. It was raining softly, and the lights of the city illuminated the clouds as they drifted just overhead. I thought of Anna, who could have been anywhere in the vast city, or beyond. I had been stupid to confront her as I did, to press her to abandon her new vows, to go so far as to sleep with her—to force her to leave. I could hardly admit to myself what I feared the most: that Barrett had summoned me to the office to tell me she was gone forever.

A loud, gruff voice behind me said, "Matt, how the hell are you?"

I turned to find Carl Barrett extending his hand. He grasped my shoulder with his free hand as we shook. He had not visibly aged since I saw him last. It was impossible to imagine Carl Barrett diminishing—any slight attenuation of the body would have been more than compensated by an increase in his air of suave confidence and capability. His face, for example, was the more dignified for the appearance of new wrinkles around his glaring eyes. His stark white hair was not the mark of approaching infirmity but the sign of distinguished achievement. His dark suit looked outrageously expensive, almost certainly bespoke, as intimidating as a suit of armor. Barrett had cultivated an appearance, an authoritarian tone of voice, a sidelong stare that left no doubt about his position or his power. In a certain light, the casual arrogance of his face could seem like brutality.

He took me into his office, which was cavernous and disconcertingly open to the outside world. Situated on the top floor, the room had a ceiling of glass that extended upward in the shape of a pyramid for twenty-five feet. The illuminated triangles were visible slicing into the sky above. Along two sides of the room were high glass walls. The view over Queens was unobstructed. Barrett's desk sat in the middle of the room, almost dwarfed by these surroundings.

"It's been, what? Two years?" he said. "What are you doing with yourself?"

"I'm teaching at a school in Harlem. Through Teach for Humanity."

"A schoolteacher," Barrett said, turning the idea over in his mind, then smiling faintly. "I can see that. I can see that. Teach for Humanity is what, a volunteer thing?"

There were layers of condescension in his tone.

"I get a small salary," I said. "This is not my final career goal."

"No, I suspect not."

He regarded me silently for a moment, resting a temple on one finger.

"What's the news?" I said. "Your secretary said you had some news for me."

He nodded and pressed a button on his phone, which whirred and beeped and, to my surprise, produced Anna's voice. It was difficult to hear her through the hissing background noise.

"Hi, it's me. I just wanted to let you know that I'm safe. Things have changed a little and Father Harrington said I needed to leave New York for a while. I can't tell you where I am or when I'll be back, but I'm okay. Remember what we talked about with the donations? Please follow through on that. I really think it would be the right thing to do. Oh, and make sure you let Matt know that I'm okay. Bye."

"What does that message mean to you?" Barrett said.

"Just what she said. Imperium Luminis moved her somewhere."

"Let me translate for you. This is a ransom message. Anna has been after me for weeks now to give money to Imperium Luminis. 'Think of all the money you have that's just extra,' she said. 'Think of all the good it could do.' I wrote her a check for ten thousand. This was a mistake. It was before I realized how ruthless these people are."

"So this is all a plot to extort more money from you?" I said.

"Listen to what she says: 'Father Harrington said I needed to leave New York for a while. Remember what we talked about with the donations? Please follow through on that.'"

"I'll tell you what really happened," I said. "A few nights ago I went to her place and confronted her. I told her Imperium Luminis had taken advantage of her. I showed her some articles about the group. The next day she was gone. She must have told Harrington I was pressuring her and he decided to move her away from me."

"Then why leave me a message and not you? Why mention the donations? Harrington put her up to this. The message is: give more money and maybe we'll return your daughter. I'll bet she doesn't even realize she's being used."

He got up and walked to the window. Resting his elbow on a bust of Thaddeus Kosciuszko, he took in the expansive view. Above us the triangles had already changed color, from sea blue to bilious yellow. From up close, the colors could be seen pulsating in intensity.

"This Gregory Blake person called me," he said. "He told me all about Imperium Luminis and how they work. I just don't understand how Anna got involved with them."

He was silent for a moment, staring into the distance.

"Are you going to donate more money?" I said.

"I'll be goddamned. Who's to say these fuckers won't keep asking for more and more?"

His tone was unexpectedly fierce, more appropriate for a street hustler than a businessman. There had been stories in the tabloids about Carl Barrett's allegedly shady business practices—huge kickbacks to the mobbed-up union bosses of the construction workers who built the Transatlantic Building, for example. Nothing was ever proved, but as Barrett fixed me with a look of ferocious defiance, I did not doubt that he was a man used to getting his way in difficult negotiations.

He reined himself in and said, "I don't intend to bankrupt myself by giving everything to these fanatics. Blake had a better idea."

He returned to his seat and rubbed his chin. He seemed to be trying to figure the best way of telling me something, considering in advance the range of my possible reactions.

"I talked to the district attorney, but she said there was nothing she could do. Anna's message is very careful not to make an explicit demand or threat. As far as the law is concerned, this is just a crazy daughter saying hello to her distraught parent. But Blake said if we knew where she was, we might be able to take her back from these people."

"Take her back?"

"It's called exit counseling. These people brainwashed her and spirited her away, so we take her back and talk some sense into her."

"But where is she?"

He raised his eyebrows and nodded. "That's where you would come in. Blake says Imperium Luminis has been trying to recruit you. Why don't you go along with it? You pretend to join them, under the condition that you be reunited with Anna. You go through their initiations or whatever. Once you know where she is, we can proceed."

Ever since Anna had dropped out of Princeton, I had been hoping for something along these lines—to be able to take her out of her increasingly desperate situation and talk some sense into her, to bring her away to some secluded place where we would be free of all distractions and complications, free to live only for each other. Maybe Barrett was right. She had gotten into a routine that was alien to the way she used to be, and the only way to help her break free was to end the routine and shock her back to her self.

"I'll think about it," I said.

On my way out, Barrett put his hand on my shoulder, a gesture that I found both gratifying and irritating.

"I know our relationship has been awkward in the past," he said. "I guess I should apologize. I've always wanted the best for Anna, and I'm a difficult man to please. But I'll tell you something—devotion counts for a lot in my book, and you've stuck with Anna through a lot of bullshit. And don't you think I don't know it."

WHEN I WENT over Carl Barrett's plan with my mother, she was strongly in favor of it. She was a child of the sixties, and as a Catholic she believed vehemently in the liberal reforms begun at the Second Vatican Council. She subscribed to a newsletter from a dissident group called the "Council of the Believers" that advocated the ordination of women as priests and a greater role for parishioners in the administration of parishes. My father called it the "newsletter from the Protestants."

In years past, my mother had led the congregation of Saint Cecilia's in folk songs on her acoustic guitar. She had told me more about her use of birth control than I ever wanted to know, simply to emphasize that it was acceptable in her eyes to call certain teachings of the Church a bunch of crap. She was, in other words, as diametrically opposed to the philosophy of Imperium Luminis as it is possible to get and still remain a Catholic.

"Imperium Luminis is a cult," she told me. "It's as simple as that. They're a bunch of fundamentalist fanatics. You have to help Anna. I always liked her so much."

"I don't want to go away with Dad in the hospital."

"Wait a little while. Until he gets better."

I called Harrington that evening and told him that I wanted to undertake the Exercises.

"Oh, wonderful, wonderful," he said. "How soon can we begin?"

"I won't be able to do them right away. My father's in the hospital."

"Just tell us when you're ready. I'll let Anna know. I'm sure she'll be thrilled."

"Will I be able to see her after the Exercises?"

"Of course."

AS EAGER AS I was to put Barrett's plan into effect, I knew that a few weeks of delay wouldn't make much difference—Anna would remain in the Light, and Imperium Luminis would still be happy to accept a new recruit. In the meantime, my father's condition was changing quickly. The doctors had lowered the steroid dose to reverse the weird psychological effects, and this modification had restored his hold on reality. But with the weaker regimen, the swelling around the tumor became uncontrolled. He grew more lethargic, sleeping most of the day. He began to slur his speech. He was receding inward before our eyes.

As I sat with him two days after I called Harrington, my father turned to me and said, "When are the Exercises?"—only the words came out deformed, sabotaged by his brain.

"How did you know about the Exercises?"

"I had a visitor last night—Anna was here."

I wondered whether I had understood his broken words. "Anna was here?" I said. "Anna?"

He closed his eyes and continued, forming each syllable deliberately, pausing frequently.

"She told me—you want to do the—Exercises. At first—I thought that you were having—a change of heart, that you—were going to—return to the Church. But then I—realized why you're doing it. You want to impress Anna. Am I right?"

"Pretty much."

"That's okay. There are worse reasons to do something—than to impress the—girl you love. Just do me a favor. Keep an open mind. The Exercises of Giuseppe Conti—are in the best tradition of the Church. Even if you don't—really want to join—Imperium Luminis, listen to what they say. You might learn something. The Lord works in—mysterious ways."

"I'm not going to do the Exercises for a while."

"Why not?"

I did not answer him. I did not want to signal what I thought was a real possibility—that he would die while I was away. He understood even without my saying anything.

"I'm not going anywhere just yet," he said. "I want you to do—the Exercises now, before you change your mind. That would make me happy."

He was becoming agitated, so I agreed to his request. Later that night I called Harrington back and told him that I was ready to join the Light.

PART TWO

NINE

FATHER HARRINGTON practically bounded across the parlor with a smile on his face when I entered the Imperium Luminis building. He was wearing jeans and a baseball cap.

"Congratulations," he said, shaking my hand. "I'm very excited for you. Are you ready?"

He indicated with an outstretched arm that I should go back outside to the street.

"I thought we would do it here," I said.

"No, no, no," he said without elaborating, leading me out to the sidewalk. Within seconds an immense white van pulled up to the curb. Harrington held open the back door for me, but I hesitated before climbing in.

"Where are we going?" I said.

"We have a place in the country we use."

This was an unexpected development, but I had already committed myself to the Exercises and, of course, it really didn't matter where they took place. I climbed inside. Despite its several rows of bench seats, the van had no windows in the back compartment. It had been built for carrying cargo and retrofitted with the seats. Harrington took the front passenger's side, next to a driver who did not acknowledge my presence.

"It's going to be a long drive," Harrington said. "It would be best if you got some sleep."

He closed a partition that separated the front seat from the cargo area. Thus enclosed, I had no view of the outside world. The van set off and was soon bouncing along the roadways of the city. I understood that they did not want me to know where they were taking me. This conceal-ment initially struck me as overkill, a move that spoke volumes about the secrecy and paranoia of Imperium Luminis, until I realized that it was designed to frustrate exactly the type of scheme I was involved in.

After a few hours the partition was opened. By that time we were on back roads, in deep forest, totally alone. Sunrise was still a few hours away. No one had said a word during the entire trip. When I got out of the van I noticed that the temperature was much cooler than it had been in the city. I wondered whether we had ascended to a higher eleva-tion. Were we in Vermont? Pennsylvania? The trilling and clicking of a thousand insects arose from the surrounding forest. In the distance was a house on a hill, barely visible against the night sky.

Harrington led me to the house, where we were met by several people, all in their thirties, all dressed in white shirts and khaki pants. They seemed unaffected by the hour. They welcomed me by my first name, smiling and shaking hands. The house was large and elegantly decorated, with mocha-colored leather couches, a marble fireplace, a grand staircase and a multifaceted chandelier.

Harrington took me upstairs to a dim hallway lined with identical doors, one of which he opened.

"You'll be in here," he said.

I waited for him to turn on the lights, but he urged me forward with his free hand.

"What about the lights?" I said, entering the room. I knew I was supposed to be in darkness for the Exercises, but I thought I might at least get a glimpse of the place before we commenced.

"There are no lights here, only the darkness. Whatever is illuminated in your time here will have to come from within yourself. The challenge of the Exercises is to forget to see with your physical eyes, to begin to see with your mind, your soul. The ability to question yourself about who you are and what you mean is uniquely human. You will have a chance to achieve your full potential, to use your mind for what it was intended. As the Benefactor says, 'If you do not know yourself you cannot know God.'"

His voice was stern and cutting. Father Harrington could have urged troops into battle. Had I disagreed with him, I was sure he would have eagerly demonstrated the full extent of my ignorance.

"So what do I do?"

"We have all the time in the world. Just relax tonight. Get used to the place. I'll be back tomorrow morning."

That first night I fought the impulse to knock on the door and politely explain that I had made a mistake. I would say that I had misjudged my own commitment and had gotten myself involved in something strange and unsettling and would prefer to be let out of the dark room.

I walked around the place, shuffling my feet and sweeping my hands before me. Each step brought the possibility of meeting a wall or knocking my shins against an unexpected obstacle. I headed toward the door, which was identifiable by a weak rectangle of light around its edges. I knocked on the door—not a desperate pounding, but three curious taps. There was no answer.

My mattress was a piece of thin foam. I tossed and turned to find a comfortable position, unsuccessfully. I told myself I was sleepy. I closed my eyes, then opened them to see if I could tell the difference.

I thought of the words of Giuseppe Conti, "You must seek the light, even in the darkness." It was such a simple thing to turn out the lights, but I saw that even an elementary act of sensory deprivation could provoke confusion, could lead someone to accept what in the light of normal life they would reject out of hand.

I was beginning to understand what they had done to Anna.

HARRINGTON WENT OVER the basics of the faith, explicating the relationship of God to the world, quoting passages and telling stories from the Bible. He related the story of Giuseppe Conti's conversion and the subsequent rise of Imperium Luminis. Breakfast consisted of water and bread, after which there was no food for what seemed an entire day. At one point I was directed to repeat a simple phrase aloud for what must have been hours.

"I am ready. I am ready. I am ready. I am ready . . ."

All of this I could handle. I could listen to Harrington for months if that's what it would take. I could skip a few meals without difficulty.

Mindless repetition of a phrase was easily accomplished; after a while I even forgot I was saying it, my mind wandering on to other matters. Just a few days in the dark, putting up with these minor hardships, and I would be able to find Anna and change the course of this whole debacle. I kept my mind focused on her, on what I would say when I found her.

Toward the end of that first day (or what I thought was the end of the first day, as I had no external time cues) the door opened and someone entered the room. Harrington had been in and out all day, so I did not take much notice.

"Matthew? Are you here? Is this the right room?"

It was not Harrington. The voice was tremulous and hoarse, suggesting an elderly speaker—a familiar voice, something from childhood, just across the transom of recollection.

"Ahhh," this person said disgustedly, stumbling into something. "These asinine dark rooms."

He sat with a heavy thump, falling into the chair with relief. He wheezed audibly for several seconds as he caught his breath.

"You don't recognize my voice, do you?" he said.

"I'm afraid not."

"It's Father Linus. Remember me?"

Of course—*that* was the voice! It sounded a little different, but it had been many years since I had heard it. Good old Father Linus, the priest who had baptized and confirmed me, who often came for dinner at my parents' house—the kindly and benevolent pastor of Saint Cecilia's who was doddering even when I was a child and must now have been truly, biblically old.

"How are you?" I said. "What are you doing here?"

"I got a call from Father Harrington that you were undertaking the Exercises. One phase of the Exercises is to talk about your family and your childhood, preferably with a priest with some knowledge on the subject. Father Harrington asked me to come up here and talk to you."

I could trust Father Linus. I wanted to reveal everything to him— how I was only pretending to be interested in Imperium Luminis to locate Anna, how I thought everyone associated with the organization was suspect. Surely Father Linus didn't approve of their tactics; in fact, he was so old that he probably didn't fully realize what was going on around him.

"I'm also here as something of a messenger," he said. "I visited with your father before I came up here. He told me that he had never really spoken to you about what happened when he came back from the war. He took my hand and said, 'Make sure you tell Matt.'"

"Tell me what?"

"Did you know that I baptized your father? Your grandparents were just another Irish family in the parish, regular churchgoers. They kept to themselves. Well, it soon became clear that your father was extraordinarily intelligent. He showed up for kindergarten at Saint Cecilia's already reading books intended for second or third graders. When he was ten, he was spending most of his class time with the eighth graders. He'd already exhausted the entire curriculum. Back then we picked out the best and the brightest to encourage them to become priests, and of course I began to push your father in that direction. We discussed Scripture and faith and his future. Once he got the idea of becoming a priest into his head, he took to it like a fish to water. He said he loved the idea of preaching sermons. When he listened to me giving my own sermons he would sit in the pew silently correcting me, working out in his head how to do a better job. He had the fervor. He said he wanted to minister to the sick and the lost. One time I even let him accompany me on my rounds to the hospital. Do you know any of this? Stop me if this is too much."

"No," I said. "I didn't know any of this."

"Looking back, I think we made a mistake with him. The possibility of the priesthood was raised too early, although he certainly seemed ready for it. But once he reached high school, what was there to rebel against? Two things—his father and his calling. One day your grandfather asked me about the church's position on corporal punishment. I told him that it was permitted if it was done in the spirit of love and if it was not excessive. You see, this was my first indication that something was changing with your father—your grandfather coming to ask permission to beat him."

I almost stopped Father Linus; this was way too much information. But I knew I had to hear the whole story. I didn't have the ability to decline this knowledge. And besides, my father had said he wanted me to hear it.

"He began to question everything—a normal part of growing up, of course, but with him it became extreme. He became enamored of existential philosophers. He would debate with me about the existence of God. A quick mind united with strong skepticism—he was strident, derisive even. He seemed extremely unhappy. When I would bring up the subject of the seminary he would just laugh. I asked him what he believed in and he said, 'Nothing.' He was hanging out with hippies, experimenting with drugs. What else could I do? He had rejected everything he used to hold so dear. He went off to Columbia and I thought I had seen the last of John Kelly."

This was an image of my father as I had not seen him before—the cynical, restless questioner rejecting his past. It was a picture, to my surprise, that reminded me of myself. Hadn't I disputed with him in the same tone, perhaps even in the same *words,* that he might have used with Father Linus?

"Go on," I said, my voice breaking slightly, betraying my stunned interest.

"At Columbia, he met your mother and performed brilliantly at his studies. There was no doubt that he would have the pick of the graduate programs in English. He had hit his stride, found his role, even if it wasn't within the Church. He had decided to become a professor. But he hesitated before picking a graduate school, and in the meantime his draft number came up. He considered becoming a conscientious objector. He even came to talk to me about it, but your grandfather would have disowned him as a coward. Anyway, your father went overseas and when he came back he was changed. The difference was extraordinary. I still remember the day he walked into my office after he returned. He was a ghost of the man he used to be. He sat down and fumbled with a cigarette, smoking nervously, looking down at the carpet. Now, I've never fought in a war. I don't claim to know much about the subject. But every time I see those TV shows about Vietnam, your father is the person I think of. That war killed him inside. It tore out his heart, his will to carry on. He was as useless as if he had gotten both his arms blown off. He told me he was tormented by nightmares, that he was terrified of going to sleep. When he was awake he was all wound up, jumpy, hypervigilant. He couldn't concentrate on anything. He was supposed to go back to school, but books seemed meaningless. He claimed to have discovered that the greatest works of literature were actually obtuse and nonsensical. They admitted him to the VA hospital on Long Island, but nothing they gave him or said helped. He came to me one night, woke me up in the middle of the night, because someone had just tried to rob him at knifepoint on the street near the rectory, and your father had not only refused to give up his wallet but had beaten the living daylights out of the guy. Your father thought he had *killed* him, but when I went to check a few minutes later the man was gone. There was a stain of blood on the sidewalk. 'I don't know what came over me,' your father said to me. I asked him what had gone on in Vietnam, and he just looked at me with a strange expression and said, 'Everything. Every eff'ing thing.' And then he began to cry. He told me that one night his platoon had been camped near a village and the villagers brought food and water to them. The soldiers went on their way, but when they came back through the village it had been burned to the ground. All the villagers had been killed as collaborators. The enemy had made an example of them, leaving the bodies all over the place—men, women and children, rotting in the dust and the heat. A few days later your father's platoon was ambushed in the jungle, presumably by the same people who had destroyed the village. Five or six soldiers were killed. The man in front of your father was shot through the throat. Then the remainder of the patrol, including your father, tracked down the ambushers, waited for night, positioned their guns around the enemy camp and opened fire. They killed everyone, maybe twenty people, just massacred them and left them there. And there was more, he said. More than he could bear to tell me."

Virtually everything I knew about my father in Vietnam came from that old faded photograph I had kept in my bureau drawer. He is posing in an olive uniform, with his sleeves rolled up past his elbows, leaning on the door of a truck. Everything in the picture is colored or tinted green—the truck, the bushes, the sky. My father is smiling, mugging a little for the camera. Whenever I asked him about the war, which was rarely, he said, "That was during a different life, kiddo. I don't want to talk about it."

"At the end of these stories, after we had stayed up all night, your father turned to me and said, 'Forgive me, Father, for I have sinned. It has been ten years since my last confession.' I told him that he was forgiven, beyond all doubt. I reminded him that he had a baby boy on the way, and that, if he sought it, he was being given a new chance by God. His penance would be to turn the evil of that war into something holy and good here at home. 'This is the first day of your new life,' I told him. And it *was*. It was a powerful thing that happened that night. I've heard thousands of confessions, but it wasn't until that one night that I truly understood the power of God's forgiveness and the change that can occur when someone accepts the gift of grace."

"We never talked about this," I said. "Him and me."

"Why should you have? The whole purpose of his new life was to be strong and to make life as normal as possible for you and your mother. He decided that your home would be a little sanctuary. The rest of the world could continue with its wars and its craziness, but inside the sanctuary your family would be safe. After a long and wandering journey, he put his trust in God, and God did not turn away from him."

Father Linus shuffled out of the room, managing to avoid the obstacles he had encountered during his entrance. The door closed and I was, once again, alone in the Exercises. Gregory Blake had asserted that Imperium Luminis went after your psychological weak spot during the Exercises. Anna had said that the Exercises simply helped you to understand who you were. I realized that both of them could be right. In the end, I did not resent or reject what Father Linus had told me. I was glad to know the truth—in fact, in the quiet darkness, turning Father Linus's words over in my mind, I was able to see my father and my relationship with him clearly, without antagonism or misunderstandings. I had been so blithely wrong about his history, about his neurotic tendencies, about his intermittent fits of anger, about his constricted ambitions, about his fierce devotion to the Catholic Church, about *him*. I felt dizzy, spiraling in the darkness. Everything was in play.

THE REMAINDER of the Exercises was a blur. Perhaps the quality of that disorienting time is best conveyed by a strange episode that occurred one day (or was it night?) just after I had woken up.

"Were you dreaming?"

I was surprised by the voice next to me, close and insistent. Harrington had been waiting for me to wake up. I did not know how long he had been sitting next to the bed.

"You were talking in your sleep, saying something about Anna. Were you dreaming about her?"

"What was I saying?"

"Her name and some mumbling. You said the word 'bobsled.'"

I racked my memory for a tracing of Anna in a bobsled, or in the snow, or something of the sort.

"What a dreary thing the unconscious mind is," Harrington said. "Here you are, an intelligent human being, but in the darkness of your mind is this stew of desires and random thoughts and instincts. In your dreams you're trapped in a nightmare world—alone and uncertain, wandering among shadows. But Imperium Luminis allows you to wake up to the light of truth."

The door opened, casting enough dim light into the room for me to see that the chair by my bedside was, in fact, empty. Someone entered with a heavy stride, closed the door and sat in the chair beside the bed, the very one I had thought Harrington was occupying.

"Good morning," Harrington said, as if we had not been having a conversation. I sat bolt upright, profoundly confused.

"Someone was here," I said. "We were talking."

"Relax," he said. "Was it a dream? Sometimes the Spirit will speak to you through a dream."

THEREAFTER everything was beyond distinct recollection. Opening doorways, insistent voices. Stories about the Benefactor. Christ in the desert. Meditate upon these things. If you do not know yourself you cannot know God. You will find Anna at a small mission in the Bronx, a place called Restoration House. You're not good enough for her at present. Can't you see the error of your ways? Why have you rejected your father? Why have you forsaken God? Who do you think you are? I know who you are. You're just a lower-class kid from Queens, dreaming of having Carl Barrett's money. Isn't that part of your obsession with Anna? You know what everyone said about you at Princeton, right? Are you ready? You are perfect in God's eyes. God has reserved for you a special place in His plan. The only way to reach the goal is through the Light. Anna is thrilled that you are accepting the Light. Anna is desperately in love with you. Are you ready? Strive to perfect yourself. Reject the shadows. Tell me your desires. Tell me your sins. Tell me your hopes. Meditate upon these things.

THE WHITE VAN took me straight from the Exercises to the hospital. I found my father lying in his bed, asleep. Although nurses and doctors were prowling the halls, he had been relegated to a remote and little-frequented room where he was permitted to rest without disturbance or intervention. Nothing more could be done for him. I walked closer to his bed. His face did not show the peace of sleep, the grateful absence of consciousness. His forehead was twisted, his mouth slightly open, a thin stream of saliva dribbling down the stubble on his chin.

I said hello, but he responded only with a guttural noise.

I found the neurologist outside.

"He can't speak anymore?" I said.

"I'm afraid not."

"Can he understand me? Even if he can't respond?"

"I don't think so."

"What's going to happen?"

"He's going to stop breathing soon. The tumor is pressing the brain from above." The doctor made a crude demonstration with his hands, one palm representing the brain and the other, curled into a fist, the tumor. "Soon it will compromise the area that controls respiration. It's called herniation. I'm afraid it's only a matter of time now."

I returned to the room and whispered to my father, "Father Linus gave me the message."

I sat down next to him. Who knows why the mind will settle on a particular memory out of a catalogue of millions? I remembered a Thanksgiving dinner when, as he stood poised with his carver over a golden bird, my father paused and looked at me and my mother with a broad smile.

"This is Thanksgiving, so I just want both of you to know that I never expected this happiness," he said gruffly. "Whatever happened before, whatever is going to happen, I want you to know how happy you both have made me."

I was acutely embarrassed. My mother looked away. All of the true import of the moment was taking place on a level above my own understanding. I wanted him to carve the turkey and stop being so un-characteristically sentimental so that we could eat. I had no idea that years later, as I sat next to his hospital bed, I would remember those words and understand them.

I thought I'd had my father figured out, when in fact all I knew was the conclusion—or, more accurately, my own *version* of the conclusion—without even an inkling of the preceding story. I was beginning to see the full scope of my errors, the extent of my self-absorption. The night was long, but when morning came I was still holding my father's unrespon-sive hand.

The Exercises were finished.

TEN

MY MOTHER ARRIVED at the hospital that morning, after making the journey that had become her special pilgrimage. She came every day to sit in silence with my father. The rest of the world had ceased to hold any claim over her; politics, commerce, the transit of people and ideas—these were all incidental to her existence, which was now focused exclusively on my father and his deterioration.

"He's coming home tomorrow," she said.

"You'll need my help then," I said.

"I can manage with Sue Donovan's help." A friend from Saint Cecilia's. "Anyway, you still need to find Anna, right?"

She took out a comb and began working it through my father's tangled hair.

"They told me where she is," I said. "Someplace called Restoration House. It's a homeless shelter in the Bronx."

"Well, you should go there."

"But are you *sure* you don't need me here?"

"What's the use of your sitting here and waiting? Besides, I want you to show those medieval bastards a thing or two."

This was about as strongly as I had ever heard my mother speak against anything. I wanted to ask her about what I had learned during the Exercises, to demand to know why she had been complicit in my father's keeping so much from me, but it did not seem proper to bring this up as we both stood over his unconscious body. To do so would have been to admit that he was finally gone, that both his history and his choices were open for new consideration.

"Just be careful," she said as I was leaving.

"What do you mean?"

"I wouldn't put anything past these people. I don't want to have to send someone up there to collect you and deprogram you."

I laughed and told her not to worry. This was the same caricature that Gregory Blake had been pushing—the evil cult of mind control, the depraved and fanatical sect. When, as the Exercises had demonstrated, the reality was so much more complicated and ambiguous.

"And leave me the number of this Restoration place," she said. "I want to be able to find you in case"—she paused for a moment, searching for the right way to say this difficult, ghastly thing—"the situation changes here."

WHEN HARRINGTON HAD told me about the "small mission" that Imperium Luminis ran in the Bronx, I'd imagined a humble soup kitchen or shelter, an outpost of charity in an area of devastation. But as I approached Restoration House I found myself wandering the leafy avenues of Riverdale, an upscale enclave perched on high cliffs above the Hudson River—a neighborhood of brick and fieldstone mansions, wide lawns, a virtual fleet of German sedans and expansive views of the river. It was near dusk and the sun had fallen to within a few degrees of the diabase Palisades on the New Jersey side of the Hudson. Golden light from inside the houses diffused into the advancing darkness. I imagined well-dressed men and women lounging in their parlors, sipping scotch, listening to Mozart, comfortable in their money. This was surely among the strangest places in the city for a homeless shelter.

Restoration House held a privileged position, directly above the river, with grounds that sloped toward the edge of the cliffs. As with the townhouse in the Village, there was no sign identifying the place as belonging to Imperium Luminis; it could have been simply the estate of a wealthy banker or broker. I approached the large iron gate and was just beginning to consider how to gain admission when, with neither warning nor signal, the gate swung open of its own accord. One of the ubiquitous video cameras was watching from above. I realized it would be difficult to get Barrett's men onto the grounds. I would have to take Anna outside and meet them at a prearranged spot somewhere down the street.

I walked toward the large white house. Anna appeared on the porch, which was lighted by glowing sconces. I could barely see her against the strong backlight. I ascended the short flight of stairs and she threw her arms around me.

"I can't believe it," she said. "This is too good to be true."

Her words were more correct than she realized. I felt a sting of guilt at the thought of what I was intending to do. Anna may have been deluded, but her happiness was genuine. She trusted me fully, and yet I was engineering a crisis that might eradicate both that happiness and that trust. My hope was that these might then be replaced by truer happiness and deeper trust, but wasn't it also possible that they might be lost forever? I was beginning to suspect that my original purpose was flawed, that Imperium Luminis wasn't as indisputably malevolent as Gregory Blake claimed it was. After all, the Exercises had turned out to be a positive and even life-changing experience. Maybe I was wrong about Imperium Luminis in general.

"This isn't really what I was expecting," I said, looking around. "It's beautiful here."

"Let me give you the grand tour."

She took my hand and led me into Restoration House.

"Father Harrington says that your Exercises were very successful."

I experienced a perverse and complicated pride; I had undertaken the Exercises solely as a means to find Anna, but I was glad to have passed the test in Harrington's eyes.

"What else did he say?"

"That you learned more about yourself, that you saw your life in a new way. The Light is a gradual thing, but he says you're well on your way now."

We walked into the mansion. A fire was crackling in a marble fireplace, casting shifting light across the herringboned wood floor. Heavy red curtains with highlights of golden thread hooded the tall windows. The sofas and chairs seemed to have been upholstered with medieval tapestries.

"I know, I know, when I first got here I thought this was an odd place for a shelter, and an odd way to decorate it," Anna said. "But that's just the thing—Restoration House is so much more than an ordinary homeless shelter. Everywhere else in the city the shelters are just warehouses. They perpetuate people's dependency. Imperium Luminis came up with a totally different approach. Restoration House is where we turn people's lives around. We take people from dire situations and let them live here for a few months. Our doctors treat their addictions and manage their withdrawal. Our psychiatrists counsel them. We give them serious job training. We help them find jobs. We help them find housing. When they leave, they're ready for the world in a way they weren't before. This is one-stop shopping for a better life."

"And when they leave they're members of the Light?"

"Not necessarily. But many are."

Anna took me through the building, which was large and pristine. Each upstairs room had been renovated in a spartan modern style, with blond wood and brilliantly white furniture. Anna showed me the seminar rooms used for group counseling sessions. We passed through a small hospital ward, complete with a nurse's station and multi-colored syringes and beeping monitors. ("For treating drug and alcohol withdrawal.")

The job-training center included a computer room with state-of-the-art machines where, she said, the residents learned programming and web design.

"You'll have to meet Justin, our computer teacher. He used to work at Microsoft before he joined the Light. He can make a computer do absolutely anything."

"This must have cost a fortune," I said, running my hand over one of the computers.

"Our members are very generous. I can't think of a better place to donate money to. We've helped thousands of people."

"So where are all the residents?"

"At dinner," she said. "Are you hungry?"

On our way downstairs, I asked how they had decided to use that particular building.

"A member willed it to Imperium Luminis. Restoration House started ten years ago in a run-down building in Harlem with plaster falling down and vermin and everything else. What kind of message does that send about your commitment to help people? This is much better. The message is that we take the residents seriously as people, that we respect them."

"And the neighbors don't mind?"

"Why would they? We keep to ourselves."

The dining hall, a long room with several rectangular wooden tables, was enclosed mostly in glass, providing a view over the river that included, at that moment, the last traces of the sunset. There were perhaps forty people in the room, of mixed ethnicity and race, eating and engaging in subdued conversation. The men were clean-shaven and had short haircuts. The women had pulled their hair back into buns. The most striking feature of the scene, however, was the fact that everyone was wearing the same outfit—a white button-down shirt and khaki pants. I realized that Anna was wearing the same ensemble. I felt suddenly conspicuous in my jeans and dark shirt.

I helped myself to pasta and salad from a buffet along one side of the room. Anna sat next to me, slightly apart from the residents. I noticed that she was eating only bread and butter.

"It means so much to me that you're here," she said. "I hope you're as happy here as I am."

CURFEW CAME AT nine o'clock at Restoration House and, having nothing better to do, I picked up a copy of *The Pilgrim* that had been left on my bedside table. I turned idly to the chapter about Giuseppe Conti's conversion:

Thus I retreated to the inner mountains of the island. I did not know where I was going or why I was going there; I only knew that the life I was leading was intolerable and that something better lay waiting for me somewhere in the wide world. I shaved off my mustache to disguise my identity. I hitched rides on the infrequent trucks and donkey carts. I walked countless dusty miles, sweltering under the oppressive and unrelenting sun. I opened myself to the workings of chance, on the theory that if God was in fact directing events then the machinations of chance would lead me to my destiny, indeed to the fulfillment of His will.

How can I convey the glory of that landscape? It was somewhat shocking to me. I had spent most of my life on the coast near the town of Sciacca, over which my family had long held its malignant influence. There was the usual danger from common thieves who haunted the interior of the island, and an even greater danger from professional kidnappers who might attempt to seize a member of the family for ransom, knowing that the Contis could well afford to purchase a safe return. I convinced myself that I was safe; I made myself anonymous, changing my appearance. I was finally free of the burden of expectations, the weight of my family history, the knowledge that my numberless enemies might be plotting against me. I called myself Salvatore. If anyone asked for my full name or inquired about my family, I said that I was an orphan and a foundling, looking for honest work. I made my way toward those remote and sublime mountains by stops

and starts, finding work as a day laborer and grape picker. I was always provided for by my fellow countrymen, who were generous with what little
they had. I lost track of the days, and then of the weeks, and finally of the
months, until my old life was as a dream half-forgotten in the serenity of
morning.

The winds of chance brought me to Castelbuono, a tiny hamlet on the
slopes of the Madonie range. It felt, by the time I reached Castelbuono, that
I had been traveling for years, that I had surely reached a destination of some
sort; indeed, it was literally the end of the road because the road went no farther, but led directly into the high country around Castelbuono—fierce and
rugged limestone crags, a landscape from the very edge of the world, from
one of the lonely places of the earth.

I explored the isolated town, asking everyone I met for work. One man,
thinking that I was a beggar, gave me some money; I swallowed my wounded
pride because I was hungry and he had given me enough for a full dinner.
When I saw him the next day I said, "Thank you for your kindness, sir, but
you were mistaken. I am not a beggar. I only want to work."

He asked my name and where I came from. I gave him my speech about
being an orphan. He looked me over and seemed to debate within himself
as to my character and strength. Finally he said:

"My family tends sheep in the mountain pastures above town."

He pointed vaguely toward sharp and precipitous peaks that seemed an
unlikely place to raise sheep.

"We could use some help."

I nodded.

"The trails are so difficult that we have built a small hut on top of
one of the mountains. We need someone to live in that hut and watch the
sheep in the most remote pastures. It means you would not see anyone for
days at a time."

The man seemed to think that this was a difficult assignment, and that I would lose interest once I heard about the isolation. On the contrary, the thought of that seclusion, that solitude, struck me as ideal. Had I not been running from the world, fleeing the evil of my life, searching for comfort and protection and enlightenment? I craved some time to myself with no interruptions, no external concerns—an opportunity for moving further inward, for meditation, for peace, for exercise of the soul.

The next day I set off for the mountains with my employer and a burro loaded with supplies. In my sack I carried the tattered copy of the Bible given to me by the itinerant preacher in Messina.

I FOUND ANNA lounging in the library the next morning, reading a book called *Faith, Hope, Love: The Teachings of Giuseppe Conti.*

"Why did you go to see my father?" I said.

She looked up from the book and said, "Father Harrington wanted you to undertake the Exercises as soon as possible. We wanted your father to encourage you."

"Well, he did."

"He seemed very supportive of your decision to join the Light."

The library was lined with thousands of books—cloth spines, antique lettering, exquisite editions. I picked a book off the shelf and fanned the pages with my thumb, expecting that the entire library was a sham, that the books were filled with blank pages.

"Why don't you talk to me?" she said.

"What's there to talk about?"

"I know his condition is only going to get worse. How are you doing with this?"

"Fine."

I was determined to keep myself under control. She pulled me down onto the couch next to her.

"Seriously, I want you to talk to me."

"He's dying."

She recoiled at the word, or at the tone in which I said it.

"God has a plan," she said. "We might not see the larger implications now, but we have to put our trust in God and realize that there is a higher purpose to this suffering. Do you believe that?"

She looked at me with her large, dark eyes. Once again I was amazed by her faith, her innocent trust in a benevolent universal scheme. She seemed to be giving me permission to drop all artifice, to level with her and release my starkest emotions.

I kissed her on her lips and returned to my room, where I threw myself onto my small bed and thought of my father. I imagined him— immobile, unconscious, gagging on his own saliva. I thought of all that Father Linus had told me. I recalled how harshly I had dismissed my father when I returned from Sicily, and at other times as well—questioning his sacrifices, not understanding what it had taken for him to recover from the war and become a father to me. How I wanted to speak to him again! I blamed God for arranging events in such a way that I could only glimpse the truth about my father's past after I could no longer discuss it with him. I blamed God for planting those horrible, polymorphous cells within my father's brain. The world itself, I thought, was a glioblastoma multiforme—malignant, unfettered, ultimately fatal. Anna could not be right about God's plan, or God's existence, because if God had conceived any of this then he was obviously a sadist, a ruthless maniac.

For the first time since I had seen my father's body begin its fierce disobedience, shaking and convulsing in the grips of that seizure, I indulged myself in tears. The fact that I was at Restoration House seemed to put me at a distance from events on the outside, so that my emotions were no longer constrained. I cried alone and desperately.

The route was astonishingly difficult. Although I had been walking the countryside for months and performing the most back-breaking physical labor, still I had to struggle to climb that ancient trail. The beginning required what appeared to be a nearly vertical angle of ascent. The burro brayed and tossed his head in refusal. My guide took out his whip and lashed the recalcitrant beast, who then resumed a slow, staggering ascent.

We passed through verdant meadows where the sheep grazed—small, rock-strewn fields delimited by lofty limestone outcroppings. Still the journey continued. I hesitated to stop, for fear that my guide would commence to lash me like the burro. The air was changing, becoming cooler and scoured by the wind.

"How did you choose this place, of all places, to raise your sheep?" I said, fighting for breath to form the words.

"This land has been in my family for hundreds of years. It is good pasture, only difficult to reach. Actually, I hardly even notice the climb anymore." Then, understanding my distress, he paused for a drink of water.

"It's not much farther," he said. "The hut is just over that peak."

He was pointing to a massive, sharply serrated body of rock. Its face seemed vertical, looming above us, high and remote and barren.

Onward. The burro's knees almost buckled, earning the overloaded animal another lashing. Each step, each movement of my own feet required conscious resolution and direction. What had I gotten myself into? What could possibly be the point of this arduous journey? Would whatever I was

going to find at the conclusion be worth this struggle, this torment? In my
weakness, I imagined my life as it would have been had I not set out on my
insane, directionless pilgrimage. The comfortable villa of the Conti family.
Attentive servants to see to my every desire. The never-ending embrace of a
succession of beautiful women—

The braying of the donkey pulled me out of my daydream. We reached
the hut, a small wood-and-stone shack situated in a relatively flat meadow,
overlooking the Mediterranean Sea in the distance. My questions about the
utility of the journey were instantly answered. That remote field—with its
multitude of wildflowers and white cliffs and the calm, infinite ocean—
was one of the most beautiful places in which I had ever found myself. The
sense of solitude was extreme. The only sounds were the crunching of my
guide's footsteps, the relieved snorting of the burro and the moaning of the
wind as it blew through the surrounding canyons—and the first two of those
sounds, I knew, would soon be gone. I experienced a momentary fear that,
alone in that sublime and fearsome landscape, I would lose my mind. I dis-
missed the thought. I knew already that my time on that mountain would
leave me changed in some profound way. I felt the coming of Your grace, O
Lord, and my heart was full.

THIS WAS ANNA as I had never before seen her. Harrington was
technically in charge, but his duties at various other locations tended to
pull him away from Restoration House. Anna functioned as his deputy.
She roamed the halls, asking questions of everyone, rearranging sched-
ules and overseeing bureaucratic details. When there was a small flood
in a downstairs bathroom, she was the first one summoned and the one

who dealt with the plumber. She approved expenses and signed the checks. When new residents arrived she would greet them and, in a firm yet caring tone, explain the house rules. I had never seen Anna in a position of authority. It struck me as a strange paradox that in Imperium Luminis, where she was in some ways totally bereft of autonomy, she had gained a new authority, a new voice.

I passed her office one day and listened to her on a phone call.

"Yes, I'm calling on behalf of Walter Jones.—I'd like to arrange for a change in the visitation rights for his son.—Yes, I'm well aware of what the settlement says, but there has been a fundamental change in Mr. Jones's living situation.—Look, we can either reach an amicable agreement with your client, or we will petition the court for a new hearing. Either way, Mr. Jones *is* going to be able to see his son. Our lawyers are very good, you know.—Yes, please get back to me as soon as possible."

I knocked on the doorjamb and entered the room.

"Working the phones?" I said.

"I should have been a lawyer."

She was sitting in a leather chair behind a large wooden desk. Through the window and a curtain of leaves was a view of the placid river. She stretched her arms toward the ceiling and yawned, then put her feet up on the desk.

"Maybe I *will* be a lawyer," she said meditatively.

"Is there that much litigation involved in the Light?"

"You'd be surprised."

"Imagine what Carl Barrett would think. After everything, you turn out to be a lawyer."

"You think he'd approve?"

"You still haven't told him where you are, have you?"

"He doesn't understand the Light. The last time I spoke to him he had been in touch with Gregory Blake, who had filled his head with all sorts of nonsense and misrepresentations."

"Your stepfather contacted me, you know. He said you had asked him for money."

She paused for a second and regarded me suspiciously. I wondered if I had said too much, if my tone had revealed my disapproval.

"That's right. Think about it—with a million dollars, which would really be like pocket change to him, we would be able to open another Restoration House in a different city. But of course he said no. I'll get back in touch with him eventually, when the time is right."

She turned to gaze out the window. The set of her face reminded me of Matteo Damiani—the faraway expression of an artist lost in thought. I asked her about her father.

"I've actually been writing to him. He's not a huge fan of Imperium Luminis, but I think he's pleased that I decided to join an organization with roots in Sicily. I swear, I think if I joined the Mafia he would be proud that I valued my heritage."

"When was the last time we talked like this?" I said. "Just sitting around and talking?"

"It feels good, doesn't it?"

"Comfortable. Perfect."

Later that night, I sat at dinner with a man who introduced himself as Walt. I asked him what he thought of Restoration House.

"It's like I died and went to fucking heaven—oh, excuse me. Got to watch that around here, right?"

He was a tall, thin man with the eyes of an overexcited child; they roved around the room, as though he had not yet fully accommodated to his surroundings. We were both dressed in the white shirt and khaki uniform.

"How did you find out about this place?" I said.

"I got here because that girl, Anna, she saved my life."

He stopped and nodded for emphasis.

"How?" I said.

"I was riding the subway, going nowhere, just killing time, wondering where I would get the money for my necessities, and she comes up to me and starts talking about God, and I said I wasn't interested, and she tells me that I'm not a bad person for everything that I'd done and that there's still hope, that there's always hope, and then, for some reason, I don't know why, maybe I was just bored, but I started listening. She asks me what's my name and where I'm from. There was something in her voice, something in her face, that just made me trust her, you know? She brought me up here that afternoon. I couldn't believe this place. I thought, even if nothing else good comes out of this, at least I'll get to pretend I'm on *Dynasty* or something. But Anna's the best. I owe her so much. I love her, in a way—not as man and woman, but as a person."

"Are you going to join Imperium Luminis?"

"Absolutely. I'm going to do the Exercises just after I leave Restoration House. Anna said I was doing drugs because something was missing in my life, and I agree with that. I believe that God saved me. I feel it on a deep level. I want him to fill my emptiness. Because if it wasn't God who saved me, then who did?"

After dinner, Anna and I played a game in which the board represented life. Our markers progressed across its fictional world. We drew cards that directed us to receive raises, lose our jobs, buy houses, sell cars, have children, get sued and so on. As our proxies journeyed across the board, I looked around at the elegant parlor where we were sitting. Anna was happy, shaking the dice with gusto and reacting to setbacks in the game with mock agony. I thought: Why not stay here? Imperium Luminis is doing good work at Restoration House. Anna has found herself in a way I could never have anticipated.

The good places to land on the board were few and far between, surrounded by traps and impediments. Maybe, I thought, the trick to the game was to recognize the good places and remain there.

On the night of my arrival, the lonesome and exposed nature of my new position was demonstrated by a thunderstorm of cataclysmic proportions that rolled through the mountains. I had barely gotten my supplies inside the building when the world grew dark and cool. A clap of thunder—louder than any I had ever heard, so loud that it seemed to break around or within me, not above me—shattered the peace of the valley.

I spent that night cowering in the drafty hut as the larger world fell apart with shuddering crashes. Rain poured through small gaps in the roof, and after some time I was as wet as if I had remained outside in the storm. I thought longingly of the Conti villa. I had finally reached the polar opposite of my former life, all the qualities of which were negated or inverted in that humble and inadequate shelter. Had a bolt of lightning struck me up there, taking my life, who would care about it, or even hear about it? My boss would return in a week with the burro loaded with more supplies; he would find my singed and lifeless body; he would bury me right there in the field, the trouble of hauling the weight down the mountain being too onerous, even for the burro; he would mention my passing to a few people in Castelbuono, and that would be the end of it—no obituaries, no wailing in the Conti villa, no gnashing of the teeth (or even surreptitious celebrating) in the streets of Sciacca. I had sought to make myself nothing, and I had achieved my goal. I felt that I was on the verge of slipping into the ranks of the anonymous dead. I fell asleep to the clatter of the rain and the gradually dissipating booming of the storm, like an army retreating from a battlefield.

When I woke the next morning, the storm was gone and the sun was shining brilliantly. The world had been scrubbed clean. To my surprise, one of my new charges had stuck his head through the door of the hut and was regarding me curiously. I scrambled to my feet and looked out the window, where perhaps a dozen sheep were milling about.

My job was quite simple. I led the sheep from pasture to pasture by means of a long staff, quick feet and nearly constant hectoring and cajoling. These infuriating animals demonstrated to me the true meaning of stupidity. I did not begrudge them their unthinking, unblinking progress through a given day, but I did resent their utter inability to realize my intentions and to act accordingly. My beloved dog back in Sciacca often seemed to know my will better than I did, to have internalized my wishes and expectations. Those idiotic woolly animals, on the other hand, had no clue as to what pasture they should be in, or where I was leading them, or why. In directing them I resorted to knocking them with my staff and cursing them, to which they would respond with agitated bleating.

Aside from leading the sheep around, there was not much to do on the mountain. I grew a long, prophetic beard. My only reading material was the Bible I had brought along, which had been given to me by the preacher in Messina. As the sheep went about their mindless business, I would spend the day perched on a sun-warmed rock, reading of the Israelites and the Apostles. To my surprise, it was enjoyable, engaging and occasionally scandalous. I immersed myself in that universal story, from the first page to the last, and when I had finished I looked up toward the heavens and said:

"O God, what is the matter with You? If what is written here is true, then You have abandoned us."

The sheep looked up at me, chewing their weeds.

"The world is corrupt, ruled by geniuses of evil and war! The murderers and criminals are reigning triumphant! Everywhere, the ceremony of the past is discredited! Your name is reviled and spat upon!"

I was working up a head of steam. I stood and shouted at the very top of my voice.

"The suffering is unimaginable! Millions butchered in the Great War like animals in a slaughterhouse, and to what purpose? And now we stand on the verge of another war in Europe, with millions more lining up for the guillotine! We are raping the land, raping each other! The innocence of the past cannot hold—something baleful and malignant is creeping into the world! The rivers are running red! The world is descending from chaos to chaos! If You love us, if You exist, why won't You help us? Help us!"

There was, of course, no answer from above. I took the sheep in for the night and returned to the hut.

THE NEXT DAY, I received a visit in my room from Father Harrington. He did not knock before he entered.

"I see you've been reading *The Pilgrim*," he said, running his finger over the copy of the book that lay open on my desk. "Good, good."

"Anna and I once visited that hut in Sicily."

"I know. But that was before you had any idea of the glorious revelations that took place there. What else have you been reading?"

"Nothing right now."

"Well, how about before you arrived here? What was the last book you read?"

I thought for a moment.

"*Degradation,* by Victor Eames."

Harrington widened his eyes in surprise, as though I had said I was reading the work of Dr. Seuss.

"That nihilist? That pornographer? There is nothing to his writings, no truth."

"He's a Nobel laureate."

"You should stick to *The Pilgrim* from now on. There is no sense wasting your time reading garbage."

He lowered his voice and leaned closer to me.

"How has it been being here with Anna?"

"Wonderful."

"Has she made any sexual advances toward you?"

Unfortunately not.

I said, "No, of course not."

"And how about you? Have you felt yourself attracted to her in that way?"

I was becoming increasingly uncomfortable. It would have been simple to deny any such impulses, but I was curious to hear what he would say if I admitted the truth.

"Every time I see her," I said.

He nodded and patted me on the back. "Good. It's healthy to acknowledge these things. But the body must be controlled. The desires of the flesh cannot be allowed to dominate our thoughts. We are more than animals, and we must always strive to act like our better selves."

I nodded, thinking that our little talk was over. Instead, Harrington said, "Roll up your sleeve."

I did as he instructed. He produced a small bracelet that seemed to have been made of thin barbed wire—the dreaded circlet. Without a word, he encircled my upper arm with it and closed the clasp. A searing pain shot through the region as the barbs entered my skin.

"You will wear this for three hours every day, until you have disciplined yourself."

As soon as he left I took the thing off and held a tissue to the area to stop the bleeding.

I went outside and passed a group of residents praying in a room down the hall. They were kneeling and murmuring in candlelight, their heads bent over their clasped hands, expressions of angst and intense focus flitting across their faces. Were these residents of Restoration House crazy, or was I wrong to question their fierce devotion? I thought to myself that an atheist and a believer, given an infinite amount of time and unlimited knowledge of world history and human psychology, would be unable to debate the question to a resolution, and in fact would probably come to blows.

Just as I was about to turn away, the group of worshippers erupted into song. They held hands and formed a loose circle. Swaying and singing words I did not understand, they began to dance—first in a clockwise direction, then counterclockwise. Their song was ecstatic, and their expressions were radiant with joy and trust. They seemed to have been transformed into children. One of the residents saw me at the door and waved her hand, inviting me to join the romping circle. I refused at first, but she left the circle, took me by the hand and brought me to the group. I had no idea what they were singing. I had no idea which way to move. But I soon lost my initial embarrassment and dropped my pose of ironic detachment. I started to laugh and smile and dance along with them.

That was the fateful night, the night toward which my entire life had been leading. I climbed into my bed, still in a dark mood. It was a peculiar effect of that extreme isolation that I could be put into a depression by an abstract meditation on the state of the human race, but that was, nevertheless, the case. It was something of a personal matter as well—for if I had not left Sciacca, would I not have been one of those eagerly engaged in murder and evil? And since I had renounced that life, what was left for me? To sit on a desolate mountaintop and brood over the triumph of injustice while tending to a flock of obtuse animals?

My frenzied thoughts sank into incoherence, and then, in the course of the night, ascended back into splendid coherence.

For in the depths of that night I was awakened by a knock on the door. Expecting to find my employer but puzzled by his chosen hour of arrival, I quickly lit a candle and opened the door to admit him. I was surprised to find a stranger, who nevertheless looked somewhat familiar. He was a large man, and he carried a cloth bag over his shoulder. He fixed me with his gleaming, deep-set eyes. Where had I seen him before?

"I am sorry to bother you," he said. "I am lost and I need shelter."

I glanced at the surrounding landscape, which was entirely hidden by the darkness. It was a new moon. Had I stepped away from the small candle I had lit, I would not have been able to see anything at all.

"How did you get here?" I said. The climb to the hut was difficult in the daylight, but surely impossible in the dark. The man did not answer.

I guessed that, although the hour was late, the stranger might be hungry, so I let him in and gave him some bread and a small glass of wine.

"What is your name?" I asked. He did not answer.

"Are you a beggar, then? A tramp?"

He kept silent.

I shrugged and was about to return to bed when he said, "I was nearby when you made your little speech today. Complaining and appealing to God for help. Have you ever thought about the way in which evil enters the world?"

"It is inevitable."

"It is not inevitable. It is the result of a million decisions to join and further the darkness. It is a giving in to a seduction. And where is the force in the world that would oppose this darkness, this seduction? A force that would fight it as an army fights a hated enemy?"

The man spoke with charismatic authority. It was then that I recognized him. This was the itinerant preacher who had given me the copy of the Bible in Messina. I was also aware that he was something more.

He continued:

"The Church needs reform. It is weak and corrupt, ruled by hypocrites and powermongers who shrug at injustice when they are not themselves participating in it. No, what we need is a group of dedicated servants to sanctify the world—an army of the faithful. An Empire of the Light. Only when we begin to pursue the Good with the same energy and passion with which others pursue evil will we achieve the reign of peace. Only then will we live in the Empire of Light."

Soon thereafter, I was overcome by sleep. I dreamed of the stranger's words—"The Empire of Light"—which my liberated imagination automatically translated into Latin: Imperium Luminis. The letters glowed brightly in my mind; letters of fire. I dreamed that in every corner of the world that name was spoken with reverence and delight. I dreamed that the hungry were fed, the homeless sheltered, the lonely comforted, the angry pacified, the hopeless encouraged, the debtors forgiven, the revengers satisfied, the imprisoned released, the doubters convinced, the addicted sati-

ated. All was possible! Nothing was unattainable! I woke to a brilliant day with a strange phrase echoing in my mind: "The City of Man cannot stand."

I leaped to my feet, hoping to wake my guest and tell him of my long and vivid dream. But he was gone.

That morning I set off down the mountain. My sheep would manage on their own for some time. I wept in gratitude as I made my way back to the world. I wept for the evil of my old life. I wept because I realized that my long journey, in fact my entire life, had been a pilgrimage, and I was a pilgrim. My destiny had been revealed to me. I practically ran down the mountain, stumbling in my eagerness to start my work.

Something new was coming into the world through me.

WANT TO TAKE a walk?" I said.

Anna checked her watch.

"Dinner starts in ten minutes."

"So we'll be a little late. Come on. It's a beautiful evening."

She glanced out the window and looked at me like I had lost my mind.

"It's raining."

"Well, it must be my old Irish heritage talking. I think it looks great out there. Look at how the leaves are shimmering in the rain. Look at—"

"Okay, okay," she said. "Let's get some umbrellas."

It was indeed raining, and although it was crucial that I get Anna outside, I had not been lying when I said the evening appealed to me. The grounds of Restoration House were shrouded in a thick fog; the trees and bushes and the house were hazy ghosts of themselves.

The rain was a mist that saturated the air and fell gently upon every surface beneath.

"So this is what Ireland is like?" Anna said. "Give me Sicily any day. Ugh."

"I finished *The Pilgrim* last night."

This piqued her interest. "What did you think?"

"I think the Benefactor had his heart in the right place. I think he truly believed that Imperium Luminis could remake the world."

"And you think it can't?"

"I think the world is a difficult place to remake."

We came to the edge of the property, the cliffs that sloped down to the river below. We spent a few moments looking out over the Hudson, upon which clouds of mist were dancing.

"Let me ask you something," I said. "What is the plan? I mean, here I am, trying to understand Imperium Luminis. I came to Restoration House. I did all this for you. So what's going to happen to us now?"

"We're going to be married," she said, as if I had proposed to her and forgotten about it.

"We are?"

"Absolutely. When Father Harrington thinks the time is right. We'll spend the rest of our lives as members of the Light, traveling the world, doing God's work."

"And what if I didn't want to do God's work. Say five years from now we just want to settle down and have kids and live a normal life?"

"Define 'normal,'" she said, but her tone indicated that such an ordinary aspiration was beneath her.

I tried to gather my thoughts, to cobble together my resolution. I had been putting off the inevitable decision, agonizing as I lay in bed at night, and now the time had come. This was the day and the hour that I had chosen with Barrett. Outside the gates were the men who would whisk Anna away to Montauk, away from Imperium Luminis. All that was left was to betray Anna. But as she spoke of marriage and the future, I found myself hesitating. The doubts and questions made another round in my thoughts. Restoration House had turned out to be a relatively benign place. There, more than anywhere I had ever been, Giuseppe Conti's vision of a better world was being made real. I was discovering new and wonderful things about Giuseppe Conti and the Light every day. Anna was comfortable and happy. It seemed that if we aborted our walk it *might* be possible for us to have a normal life together under the auspices of Imperium Luminis.

We strolled along the inside of the tall wrought-iron fence that surrounded the property. When we reached the front gate I still had not made up my mind. I pushed Anna's umbrella out of the way and kissed her. I placed my hands on her hips.

"Why are your hands shaking?" she said.

I ran my hand up her arm and there it was. I rolled back the sleeve of her shirt and found the circlet. The barbs were buried in her skin, which had become red and puffy in response to the abuse. It reminded me of the IV catheter that had taken up permanent residence in my father's arm. My decision was made.

"Let's keep going," I said, releasing her arm. "I want to walk around the neighborhood."

"You know we're not supposed to leave without a reason."

"There *is* a reason. I'm getting a little stir-crazy in here. Wouldn't it be nice just to walk around and look at the houses for a few minutes? Or go to the deli down the street and get a bagel or something?"

She shrugged and said, "You can go ahead."

"No," I said, a little too abruptly. "I just want your company." I put my arm around her. When I felt her body relax into mine, I knew she would go along with me. She punched a code into a keypad on the fence and the gate swung open.

We walked a block. I told myself that I was doing the right thing. I tried to restrain myself from grabbing her and running ahead to the pre-determined corner, simply to get it over with. It seemed it took us an hour to reach the corner. I was aware of every noise, every splash of stray raindrops into puddles, waiting for the sound of the cars behind us. Anna asked me a few questions but I was too nervous and excited and guilty to speak.

It happened quickly. A squealing of tires as two sedans pulled up next to us. Anna tensed and grabbed my hand so hard that her nails nearly broke my skin. "Run," she said, but the men from the first car were in front of her. They were brawny guys in suits emerging from sedans with tinted windows, and anyone watching the scene would have thought it was a mob hit.

I allowed myself to be shoved into one of the waiting cars. The driver leaned back and said, "Good job." As we pulled away, tires screeching, the men were on the verge of successfully corralling Anna into the back seat of the other car. Local residents were standing on their stoops, amazed, struck dumb by the scene. One man was speaking into a cordless phone, no doubt calling the police.

And Anna was struggling and shrieking and saying, "No, don't do this. This is so wrong. Please don't."

ELEVEN

THE CAR PROVIDED by Barrett was quite luxurious, a Mercedes with deeply padded leather seats and a small plasma-screen television in the back seat. More out of a sense of novelty than interest, I flipped around the channels for a while. I paused on the adventure channel, which was presenting a show about avalanches. I watched a video clip shot by a man climbing in Nepal. He is shooting film of the peak above him when he notices a white cloud silently arising from the very top of the mountain. He says, "Oh my God," but does nothing. He keeps the video camera trained on the white cloud, which is becoming larger and closer. A faint rumble is audible in the background. It is mesmerizing to this man, an avalanche of vast proportions tumbling down the mountainside. It looks pillowy soft, as harmless as a cumulus cloud. The man has apparently concluded that he cannot run from the avalanche, so he simply keeps filming. Is he turning over in his mind the innumerable decisions that brought him to that place at that time? As the end approaches, can he even think at all? At the last second, just as the snow has darkened the sky above him and is about to engulf him, the images on the screen jump and waver as the man runs inside his tent. He turns the video camera to his own face, which is contorted in a wince of anticipation. Chunks of ice are heard raining down on the tent, and after a moment all is quiet. The camera whips around again as the man unzips the tent and emerges, his tent almost buried, into a new world of pristine snow. He shouts and tosses the camera aside. We see him dancing and frolicking in the snow. He seems to have been driven insane by his brush with death. He has been saved.

I looked up from the screen and saw that we were passing through the Upper East Side of Manhattan. I glanced into the surrounding cars, looking for the one carrying Anna, but all I found were speeding taxis. I caught a glimpse of my old high school, Saint Brendan's, a fortress of a building with large granite columns. Two blocks farther downtown we passed Anna's old school, Notre Dame (pronounced with a French accent), which was housed in an elegant townhouse off Fifth Avenue.

Saint Brendan's was a scholarship school for Catholic boys. It had been founded around the turn of the century when a wealthy Protestant woman, noticing that her Catholic servants had no superior school for their children, bankrolled such an academy in her neighborhood. The boys of Saint Brendan's came from the provincial hinterlands, and traveled into the city by subway from Bensonhurst and Bay Ridge and Bayside. Gaining admission was fiercely competitive, with only a few dozen spots available and an entire city of lower- and middle-class Catholic parents hoping and praying for their sons to be chosen. It was well known that most Saint Brendan's boys went on to win scholarships to the Ivy League.

Saint Brendan's was surrounded by the private schools where the rich and powerful of the city sent their children. This was how I met Anna. Since Saint Brendan's was an all-boys' school, almost any dramatic production short of *Waiting for Godot* presented a problem of accurate representation. When Saint Brendan's needed girls to play female roles, we invited students from Notre Dame, just down the street. One afternoon, as I was walking through the halls on my way home, I passed a stunning girl in a plaid skirt with long curly hair who was looking around as if trying to find her bearings.

"Can you tell me where the auditorium is?" she said.

There was something riveting about her brown eyes, which were staring at me with such intensity that for a moment I thought I had not heard her correctly, that she had asked me a more serious and complicated question. She narrowed her eyes suspiciously, wondering what could be wrong with me.

"It's this way," I said, beginning to walk with her. "I was just going there myself."

"Are you trying out?"

"Definitely."

"For what part?"

I should have known better than to lie. I didn't even know what play they were casting. I considered abandoning the idea. Why was I being such an idiot?

"Any part," I said. "I'm not picky."

Anna auditioned brilliantly and, once I had picked up the script, I managed a passable reading. The play was *Twelfth Night,* and Anna became the shipwrecked Viola, wandering the shores of Illyria looking for her lost brother and falling in love with Duke Orsino, who was, unfortunately, not me. I played Malvolio, the dour steward, the butt of the fool's pranks.

Rehearsals became the highlight and higher purpose of my days, especially the scenes I had with Anna. I wondered whether there was any deeper meaning to the flash that came into her eyes when we read our lines—that anger, animation and life. Did she have the same look with the others? With Steven Albi, with whom, as Orsino, she was supposed to be in love? I would have limited my knowledge of the world to our one small scene together, inconclusive as it was, and not regretted the loss of all the rest.

One day, as we headed outside after rehearsal, she turned to a group of us and said, "Who wants to run lines?"

Everyone else demurred, claiming papers due and sheer tiredness. She looked at me with a questioning expression. Our lines together were limited, so the rehearsal session didn't make much sense from a practical standpoint. Nor was I such an accomplished actor that she would have wanted me around to give her pointers.

"Why not?" I said.

We emerged from the elevator onto a private landing on the penthouse floor of her building—the fabled Aurelian on Central Park West, home of movie stars and martyred musicians. The landing was not a common hallway with other apartment doors, but a small foyer offering only a single option, a door of dark wood with a golden handle. This led to the penthouse apartment itself, the main living room of which was enclosed within a two-story glass wall.

"I had a dream last night," Anna said. "I showed up for rehearsal and it turned out it was opening night and I hadn't learned any of the lines. I went out onstage and started making stuff up. And you were there, trying to feed me the right lines, but I couldn't hear you."

She tossed her backpack and coat on a couch, totally oblivious to her astonishing surroundings. I wanted to be nonchalant, to give the impression that I found myself in such apartments every day, but I couldn't stop staring out the glass wall. The view of the sky was unbroken. Down below was Central Park, a green patchwork carpet, stained with brown infields, that ran across the island and ended at the wall of gray edifices along Fifth Avenue. I thought to myself that it was a million-dollar view, but immediately realized I had undervalued it by tens of millions. This was privilege on a scale I could barely comprehend.

Who is this girl, I wondered, *and what am* I *doing up here?*

We moved aside the furniture, rolled up the rug and stood in the glass-enclosed living room, now a stage in the air. As we went through the play, doing each scene in which one of us had lines, the outside world grew dark. I watched the night coming over from Queens, a curtain descending across our stage. I was grateful for the scripts we held before us, since they relieved me of the obligation to come up with much to say on my own. We could voice Shakespeare's words, even profess undying and hyperbolic love for each other, and not reveal anything of our own ideas or intentions. I did not have to dwell on my attraction to her, or on the impossibility of our forming more than an onstage partnership when she discovered that we were from different worlds.

—"*What* is going on here?"

We both turned at the interruption. Anna's mother was standing behind the couch with her hands on her hips.

"We're rehearsing, Mom," Anna said, sullenly.

"Well, I hope you didn't scratch up the floor when you moved every-thing." Her accent—which at that point I could not identify as Sicil-ian—was prominent, rendering the words distinct and exotic.

"This is Matt Kelly, from Saint Brendan's."

"Yes, hello," she said coolly, seeming to regard me as simply another object out of place in the room. The illusion of being in Shakespeare's Illyria had been shattered. We were instead standing in a living room and Anna's mother was pissed.

"I guess we should call it a night," Anna said, sighing. "That was fun."

As I walked away from the building I looked up at the penthouse, that beacon in the night. I felt privileged simply to have been up there. Even if Anna and I never spoke again outside of the Saint Brendan's auditorium, I would always be able to find the Aurelian among the sky-line and think, that's where I told a beautiful girl that I loved her—in Shakespeare's words. Acting, of course.

Barrett's car was now speeding across the Queensborough Bridge, bringing us out of the glittering world of Manhattan and into the gritty, blue-collar neighborhood of my youth. The Transatlantic Building hov-ered behind us, its muted colors slowly dancing across its spire of trian-gles. I turned back to the TV and watched a few more avalanches, my mind wandering, remembering lines from *Twelfth Night*. I wondered what would have happened had my father not pushed for me to take the Saint Brendan's entrance exam, and had I not passed that test. I would have remained a student at Saint Cecilia's, my neighborhood parochial school in Astoria. I would never have had the opportunity to meet a wealthy girl from Notre Dame and practice Shakespeare in her lavish apartment. I would not have been subsequently dumped at the insis-tence of her snobbish parents. I would not have gone to Princeton and reconnected with her. I would never have had to consciously suppress my natural patterns of speech around her parents (less *Noo Yawk,* more like a national news anchor). I would not be, at that moment, speeding out to Long Island to convince her that she had been victimized by Imperium Luminis. Instead, I probably would have met a nice, unassuming girl from my neighborhood and gone on to become a cop, which is what most of the guys from my neighborhood had done.

And would I have been happier to have avoided all the turmoil and distress that Anna Damiani Barrett had brought into my life?

"Hey," I said to the driver. "Can we make a stop?"

MY MOTHER OPENED the door and said my name.

"How's he doing?" I said.

"He was actually talking to me yesterday. Short sentences, but he was totally with it. Today he's not so good. I tried to call you at Restoration House but they wouldn't let me speak to you. Did you get the message?"

"No. I was just on the way out to Barrett's house."

"So they got her away?"

I nodded.

"Good," she said. "Come on in already."

The living room was filled with books. The house had always been a book repository of sorts, with volumes piled high on tables and stuffed two-deep onto shelves. My father never passed a used-book sale without acquiring an armload, and new books were one of the few splurges he allowed himself. He placed various books he was reading around the house strategically, keeping in each room something close at hand. Had my father continued on his intended path to graduate school, his voracious reading would have been unremarkable, but it would also have been directed and better organized. After the war ended he became more omnivorous, reading anything that caught his interest and then stowing the book wherever it might fit. Now, to make room for the hospital bed, all the books that had formerly lodged in the dining room had been moved into the living room; the place was filled with a jumble of paperbacks and biographies.

Past the books, in the darkened dining room, he was asleep, propped up in bed with pillows. I shook him and said, "Dad."

To my astonishment, his eyes flickered open and focused on my face.

"How are you?" I said.

He seemed to understand me, but he searched in vain for a proper response. He opened his mouth, about to answer. A confused look crossed his face. He opened his mouth wider and tried again. Finally he seemed to forget the question and he closed his eyes.

"You should have been here yesterday," my mother said, leaning against the doorjamb. "He was so much better. It was sudden, just a few hours, but we got to talk a little."

"Do you want to talk?" I said to him, in a loud voice.

"No," he said, hesitantly.

"He's saying no to everything now," my mother whispered.

"Are you a Yankee fan?" I said.

"No."

I sighed and joined my mother in the kitchen. She had filled a teapot with hot water to steep.

"I'm sorry," I said. "I should be here with you. I didn't realize it was going to be like this when he came home."

"I'm managing. Sue Donovan has been helping so much. She's just a godsend."

As she filled two mugs with tea, she lowered her voice.

"So tell me about it. What was Restoration House all about?"

"Actually, it wasn't at all what I expected. I was ready for dark hallways and Gregorian chant and bizarre rituals, but Restoration House was totally different. They take homeless people and let them live there while they try to turn their lives around."

"Meanwhile indoctrinating them with Imperium Luminis propaganda."

"That's what I expected, too. But everyone who worked there really seemed dedicated to helping these people for the sake of helping them. I was very impressed. It was like they were trying to do what Giuseppe Conti said—'to sanctify the world.' It really was a wonderful place."

My mother looked at me as she sipped her tea. I took a sip as well. I always associated the warm, soothing scent of tea specifically with her.

"It seems your opinion of these people has changed," she said.

"Maybe it's not as black-and-white as I thought."

She put her tea down and leaned toward me.

"Do I need to be worried about you? Have you forgotten about all the terrible things this group does? How it preys on the weak and the confused, how it controls the thoughts of its members, how manipulative these Exercises are?"

"Actually, I thought the Exercises were helpful, in a way."

"Helpful?" she said, incredulously.

"There's a lot that you and Dad never told me. About Vietnam and when he came back."

"They brought *that* up? What right do they have to go digging around in our past like that?"

"It's not that they have a right. It's that *I* have a right. How could you not have told me what went on? The admission to the VA hospital on Long Island? I only got to hear this after Dad was too sick for me to talk about it with him. How is that fair?"

She averted her eyes and sipped her tea.

"We felt that it wasn't necessary for you to know. We were going to tell you when the time was right."

"So instead I had to hear it from Father Linus?"

She looked at me as if she couldn't quite make sense of what I had just said.

"Father Linus?" she said.

"He visited me during the Exercises."

"That's impossible. Father Linus had a massive stroke last year. He's at a nursing home for priests in New Jersey. Your father and I visited him there a few months ago. He's totally incapacitated. He couldn't walk or eat, and he could barely speak."

I put down my mug and leaned back in the chair. My mother was staring at me with a wild expression.

"Did you see him?" she asked. "You remember what he looks like. You would have been able to recognize him."

"It was dark. You're in a dark room for the Exercises."

"Well, did it sound like him?"

"I thought so at the time."

"What did this person tell you, anyway?"

"About Dad's anger. How he couldn't find himself when he returned from the war. How he almost killed a mugger near the Saint Cecilia's rectory. He made it sound like Dad had posttraumatic stress whatever. That's why he didn't go to grad school. That's why they were treating him at the VA hospital, right?"

My mother gave me a blank look and then began to laugh—a bitter, sad laughter.

"Your father," she said, leaning forward, "came back from the war addicted to heroin. *That* was why he was at the VA. *That* is what we didn't want you to know."

She maintained the same position, leaning across the table toward me with her hand outstretched. Deciding that her point had been sufficiently punctuated, she abruptly sat back and began once again to sip her tea. It seemed that her words did not hang together in the proper manner, that they were the ravings of a madwoman. I did not know which dimension of this revelation to focus on—the utter strangeness of the words *your* and *father* and *heroin* strung together in an intelligible sentence, or the plain fact that Imperium Luminis had deceived me in such a brazen and spectacular manner.

"He started using it while he was in Vietnam. Apparently there were all sorts of drugs going around over there. He said it helped him to get through—"

"I don't want to know," I interrupted, holding up my hand.

"Oh? I thought you did," she said archly.

"So nothing that they told me was true? He wasn't, you know, messed up by the war?"

"He was struggling with an addiction. Everything was pretty haywire for a few years. *That's* why he never made it back to grad school."

I stood and walked into the darkened dining room. My father was asleep with a peaceful, faraway look on his face. After some hesitation, I freed his arms from the blanket to examine them. His skin was covered with freckles and the occasional mole, but it was otherwise unblemished.

"When did it stop?" I said. My mother had taken up a position across the bed, and she looked like she was about to cry.

"It was on and off for a few years when you were very young. Methadone helped. But then he beat it. He was fine."

I looked back and forth between them.

"This doesn't change anything," she said. "What difference does it make? It's all so far in the past. What matters is what you already knew about him. What matters is how he loved you."

She was right, of course. As I stared at his recumbent form, I had the strange sensation that I did not know him, mixed with the equally strange conviction that I finally *did* know him, better than either he or I had ever intended. I stood there wondering who he was and who I was and how I could ever find out. I was seized by an anger like nothing I had ever experienced. I felt my heart surging and throbbing as if a powerful fist were contracting around it.

"They lied to me," I said. "Those fucking bastards were playing games with me. None of it was true. And I almost fell for it. How gullible can you be?"

There was nothing I could do now to help my father. Within a few days or weeks he would finish his journey. As much as I hated and feared his death, as much as I resented the absurdity and unfairness of what was happening before my eyes, so too did I hate and fear Imperium Luminis. In that instant those two entities became joined in my mind, to the extent that I actually imagined that Father Harrington—not DNA, not chance, not God—was somehow the one responsible for my father's illness. Suddenly the ramifications of Imperium Luminis were not limited to Anna and my relationship with her. I felt that if I failed to expose the truth about the group I would also be failing my father in a way that I did not fully understand.

"I'm going now," I said. "Goodbye, Dad."

He raised his eyelids but did not answer.

I went to pack a few things for the trip to Montauk. When I came downstairs, my mother was standing in the doorway. On my way out she grabbed me around the neck with her arms, pulling me into the most violent and prolonged hug I had ever been involved in. She cried quietly, her body heaving with her breaths.

The car was waiting for me outside. I walked toward it quickly, ashamed by my desire to escape from that place. By the next morning, I thought, I would be with Anna on a sandy beach, telling her all about what Imperium Luminis had done. And maybe, out of this murky circus of grief and deception, something of love and truth could emerge.

TWELVE

THE HOUSE ON Montauk was, at first glance, relatively modest, at least by Carl Barrett's standards. We approached it on a long driveway that paralleled the shore, weaving among and between the shaggy dunes. It was dark by the time we reached our destination, but the house was clearly visible in the moonlight—stark white, severe, without ornament, perched on a cliff overlooking the seething ocean. I had anticipated an extensive mansion with ivy on the walls and a grand, gabled roof, something that would declare to the world the power and wealth of its owner. As I later learned, this small white house actually announced both of these qualities, although in a more subtle fashion; the house was designed by Eric Kunstler, the celebrated architect who was also responsible for Barrett's crowning achievement, the Transatlantic Building. The house was well known within architectural circles, discussed and deconstructed in graduate seminars. Atop the roof, in a sly allusion to Kunstler's skyscraper, were several glass triangles that served as skylights.

The car rolled to a stop on the pebbled driveway. When I emerged into the night air I heard the nearby roar of crashing waves. I walked a few yards along the driveway to the edge of the cliff and looked down. There, about twenty feet below, breakers were foaming and throwing themselves against a jumble of black rocks. The night was quiet, with no hint of bad weather, but the waves were agitated and violent. During storms and hurricanes, I thought, the waves must ascend the cliff and threaten to wash away the house.

Barrett greeted me at the door with none of his usual reserve or hauteur, instead grasping my hand and slapping me on the back.

"Matt," he said. "Superb work. Everything went off without a hitch."

"Where's Anna?"

"Upstairs. With Gregory Blake."

I headed for the stairs, but Barrett said, "It would be better to leave them alone for a while, don't you think? Let the professional do his job?"

I stopped with my foot on the first stair and looked upstairs, hoping to see Anna, straining to hear her voice, but there was nothing but darkness and silence. A large bodyguard with a sidearm stood on the top step, watching me.

"Come have a drink," Barrett said. "You look like you need one."

He led me through the house, which was decorated in a modern and rigidly geometric style, such that a Teutonic robot might have been eminently at home. We descended a set of stairs into a small basement. The room had been hewn out of the rock of the cliff, and the walls were of unadorned rough stone. Along one side of the room were several stools and a small bar, with a collection of liquor bottles and glassware. Barrett stepped behind the bar and said, "What can I get you?"

I must admit that I relished the thought of Carl Barrett serving me.

"A beer would be great."

He looked mildly amused, as if he had expected me to request something a little more refined. But if he thought my choice somewhat déclassé, he said nothing as he produced a bottle of Heineken from a miniature refrigerator. For himself he poured a sizable portion of scotch, from a selection of some thirty varietals, and offered a toast.

"To a brighter future," he said. "Free of Imperium Luminis."

I clinked his glass and took an eager swig of the beer. Barrett was right about my needing a drink. As soon as I put down the bottle I felt better—less tired, less frantic, marginally less preoccupied with my father.

"So tell me about it," he said.

He gazed at me with an expectant expression. I hesitated for a moment, wondering how much I wanted to reveal to someone I had grown used to considering an adversary. I realized that we were now on the same side, even sharing a collegial drink. I told him everything. I told him how they sent in someone to impersonate Father Linus and lie about my father's past.

"They would stoop to that?" he said. I was glad to be able to tell the story from close to the beginning, and Barrett was surprisingly affable and engaged. The atmosphere was confidential. I could hardly believe that this was the man who had treated me with such disdain until just a few weeks previously. By not giving up on Anna, by entering into this plot, had I finally proven myself to him?

"Can I assume, sir, that if Anna still wants to be with me you won't object?"

He seemed caught off guard by the question, and he eyed me suspiciously for a moment.

"I'll answer that in a roundabout way." he said. "I want to level with you. What I'm about to tell you is known by very few people in the world. My given name is Karol Barycz."

He smiled oddly, gauging my reaction.

"My parents were immigrants from Poland. I grew up in Greenpoint, Brooklyn. We had almost nothing. My father worked in construction. All this"—he gestured toward the ceiling—"I have created completely on my own."

I tried to act shocked, even though Anna had already told me as much about his past. Barrett put his elbow on the bar and leaned toward me. He seemed to be inviting me further into his confidence. I was thrilled by the idea of this vastly powerful man speaking to me in such an unguarded and familiar manner. I leaned forward as well and, in that position of secret sharing, he continued in a low voice, almost a whisper:

"When the war was over and I came back from Korea I was just another skinny kid happy to be alive, looking for something to do. There were thousands of us descending on the city, clamoring for jobs, elbowing each other out of the way into the schools and universities. I knew a few businessmen from the old neighborhood who were looking to help out a war veteran, so they let me into a partnership that was buying a building—just a crappy little tenement, but they let me in with almost nothing. They put me in charge of renovating it. I poured my heart and soul into that little building, and when it was done we sold it for a return of something like fifty percent. That's how I got started in the business. A few years later I wanted to buy a small piece of land in Westchester and build an apartment building, but when I went there to meet the sellers I could tell something was wrong. They had decided against me even before I walked in the door. On my way out, one of them said, 'Hey, no hard feelings. We just wanted to bring in someone with more . . . *credentials*.' I understood exactly what he meant—they were WASPs and they didn't want to work with some low-class Polack from Brooklyn. I decided that I had gone as far in life as I could with the name of Barycz. I worked on losing my accent. I talked my way into gallery openings and such, and I studied the people. I devoted myself to the subject of money—how people who have it behave, how they speak, how they look at each other. I was an actor preparing for a role, and after a while I nailed it. I changed my name officially."

Barrett poured himself another drink. I could tell he was enjoying himself. Who knew when he had last told someone this story?

"This is all common knowledge among certain circles, of course, but I've been able to keep my story out of the press as I built my little empire. Life was very lonely until I met Anna's mother at one of Matteo Damiani's shows. Matteo was in the middle of a crowd holding forth on the symbolism of his work, and Maria was standing off to the side looking very alone and very beautiful. She spoke only Italian back then, so no one was talking to her. Her face lit up when I said, 'Buona sera.' "

He was staring into space, as if Maria Damiani were somewhere behind me.

"You see why I didn't want Anna dating you? There are people in New York who know that I'm actually new money from ethnic Brooklyn. But they go further. There are baseless rumors that fly around about my ties to the Mafia—rumors that only got louder after I married a woman from

Sicily. For Anna to be dating some kid from Queens was unacceptable. It just confirmed the worst judgment of the society types. We were thrilled when the Goddard boy took her out a few times. But, as always, Anna had her own ideas. I actually think she became fixated on you precisely because you were off limits."

"That's as obnoxious as those people in Westchester."

He shrugged. "I don't make any excuses. That's the way things work. I got to the top and now it's my prerogative."

He finished his drink and shook his head.

"You're a good kid. In a lot of ways you remind me of myself at your age."

He came out from behind the bar, slightly unsteady on his feet. He put his hand on my shoulder.

"It's all moot, anyway," he said, heading upstairs. "I doubt Anna's going to want to see either of us for a while. You should have heard her when she came in earlier, calling down the wrath of God upon me, calling me the devil."

He ascended the stairs, leaving me alone in the subterranean room. I was amazed that I had been so misled by Barrett—or Barycz. He was not exaggerating when he said he'd nailed the part; from the very first time I met him I had been intimidated by his clothes, his Anglophilia, his accent, his tone of voice, his general aura of refinement. To think that someone so eminent and distinguished could have started out with absolutely nothing, as a nobody! When Anna had first told me about his origins I thought he was a garden-variety hypocrite, but after hearing him tell his story in his own words I was strangely impressed. The truth about his background did not diminish him in my eyes. He had been the author of a spectacular revision. Dissatisfied with what he had been given, he had made himself new and invincible.

Upstairs, I found a light on in a bedroom and towels folded at the foot of the bed, apparently indicating that the room was mine. In the next room I could hear a low murmur of voices, one of them Anna's.

I went into the hallway and knocked on the door. Gregory Blake stuck his head out.

"Not now," he hissed.

"I just wanted to say goodnight to Anna."

When Anna heard my voice she said, "Is that him? Matt? How could you be a part of this? I trusted you! I *trusted* you! Let him in!"

The voice was shrill and ragged. Blake shut the door in my face. Eventually Anna quieted down and the murmuring of voices resumed. I went next door and climbed into bed. I felt alone, frightened, oddly disoriented. Everything was changing so quickly.

I WOKE THE next morning not entirely sure of where I was, confused for a few moments by the echoes and remnants of a strange dream. Directly over the bed was one of Eric Kunstler's triangular skylights, which was admitting to the room a shaft of blinding sunlight. The room, furnished in white, had taken on a brilliant, almost transcendent glow in the morning sun.

Downstairs I found Gregory Blake at the kitchen table, nursing a cup of coffee and staring out at the ocean, which looked blue and endless. Unaware of my presence, he seemed to be deep in thought, occasionally whispering to himself—rehearsing what he would say later to Anna, I assumed. The sound of my coffee cup clinking against the countertop roused him from his contemplation.

"Good morning," I said. "How have you been?"

He was in no mood for pleasantries.

"You shouldn't have knocked on the door last night. She wasn't ready for it. I know it's because I didn't have a chance to review the ground rules with you."

I took a seat across from him.

"This is a structured process, a step-by-step progression. We start with what Anna did and thought at Imperium Luminis. We tell her the truth again and again. We move backward, trying to help her understand what it was that made her susceptible to their pitch in the first place, what was missing. *That* is where you and her stepfather come in."

"Have you ever thought that this is a little bit like the Exercises?"

Blake looked at me as though I had personally insulted him.

"This is nothing at all like the Exercises. Imperium Luminis tries to distort and deceive. We undo the damage. These are the anti-Exercises."

"Of course. Sorry."

"I work from the premise that the more I know about a subject's history, the better. You went out with Anna in college, right? Why did you two break up?"

"It started when her mother died. This was junior year. Anna showed up at my door one night in tears and said that her mother had been in a car accident on Montauk and was in the hospital. It was snowing and her mother always drove here as recklessly here as she had in Sicily. Anna came out here to be with her mother."

"You didn't go with her?"

"I didn't get along very well with her family. They thought I was a little too rough around the edges for her."

"Interesting," he said.

"Anyway, her mother died on the operating table. I had no clue what to say to Anna. I wanted to comfort her, but her sadness was of a different order than anything I had ever experienced. Anna and her mother were on terrible terms right up until the end. They used to fight like cats and dogs over every possible issue. The last time they spoke before the accident, Anna had hung up the phone after shouting Italian curses into the receiver."

"So she never got to reconcile with her mother."

"When she came back to campus I was ready to comfort her. But all she said was, 'What I really want is to go get fucking hammered.' That's when the drinking began in earnest. We began to go out most nights of the week, and Anna would drink until she threw up. I thought it was something that would pass after a while, after she got over her mother's death, but it got worse. One day I found her drinking vodka in her art studio at eleven o'clock in the morning. It just kept getting more ridiculous. Eventually she was hanging out with a crowd that did serious drugs. Her painting became wild and undisciplined. She didn't come back to school the following year. The next time I saw her was just before she joined the Light."

"This is all beginning to make sense," Blake said. "Father Harrington must have had his sights on Anna for some time. She was perfect— young, rich and troubled. You really have to give Imperium Luminis credit."

IN MY BEDROOM I could hear the voices next door. I approached the wall and put my ear against it, but the words remained muffled, just beyond comprehension. Gregory Blake's voice was a steady drone. Anna would answer in sudden staccato notes in a higher octave. I went down to the kitchen and found a glass, which I took up to the bedroom and placed against the wall. With my ear against the cold bottom, I could just make out the words. Blake and Anna sounded far away, their voices disembodied, as if floating up from a submarine in abyssal waters.

"In *The Pilgrim* he says he turned his back on the Mafia, right?" Blake said.

"He writes, 'I had found a glory to which the powers of the earth and the praise of the foolish could not compare.'"

"The sad truth is that he never gave up that life. How do you think he raised the money to build the chapel in Sciacca?"

"He preached to the faithful. They recognized his greatness."

"He was extorting money, just as he did before his quote-unquote conversion on the mountaintop. He was running the same racket, only now he was saying he was doing it for God. He was no better than a televangelist."

"He's a *saint*."

"Here are sworn statements given by members of the Mafia to the Italian police after the death of Giuseppe Conti. I even have them in the original Italian for you."

"My Italian isn't good enough."

"I have them in English, too."

"You think I would believe a bunch of Mafia thugs trying to talk their way out of jail time? Over the blessed word of the Benefactor?"

There was something upsetting about the way Blake was slandering Giuseppe Conti. As much as I hated Imperium Luminis, *The Pilgrim* had struck me as the work of a genuine, if misguided, man of God. I had even been moved by his vision of a sanctified world, with the debtors forgiven and the lonely comforted and all the rest. I wanted to believe that his intentions had been pure, that whatever malignant forces had taken control of Imperium Luminis had done so only after his death. I wondered whether Anna could be right. What if everything that was taking place in that room next door was wrong?

"No one blames you," Blake said. "Imperium Luminis offered you what you were looking for—a feeling of connectedness, a sense of belonging. Answers to the way you've felt for so long, when your parents split up and your father moved to Sicily, when your mother died. You were alone and hurt and scared."

"This is about God and grace and the gift of faith. You can't explain it away with high-school-level psychology."

"Believe me, I know how you feel. Even now I sometimes look at my daughters and I think that, as much as I love them, I've paid the highest price anyone can pay for leaving the Light: I no longer know God in the same way. I'm alone, confused about what is right, struggling to raise my family. My prayers and concerns are so ordinary that I sometimes doubt that God even registers my existence. But when I was in the Light . . . That level of separation from God wasn't even there. I wasn't lost in the darkness. I was with God and God was with me and I knew truths that the rest of the world would weep to know. My purpose and God's purpose were one and the same. How could anyone give that up? I know exactly what you're going through, but there is another way."

"I know what God wants for me."

"Because someone told it to you during the Exercises?"

"I *know.*"

"No one knows. Not me. Not Imperium Luminis. Not even you. That's the horrible truth."

T H E   N E X T   D A Y Blake told me that Anna was, in his opinion, ready to see me.

"She's beginning to ask the right questions," he said. "Right now she doesn't quite know what to believe or disbelieve. She needs you to be there for her."

I paused before the closed bedroom door. A few steps down the hall stood one of Barrett's bodyguards, staring straight ahead like a member of the palace guard.

"So do you forgive me?" I said as I opened the door, but she was asleep in her bed. Usually when Anna slept she looked beautiful and peaceful, entirely relieved of the burdens and worries of her waking life, but now she looked distressed. She was sleeping with her mouth half open. Her skin was pale. A thick blanket covered her to the chin, and she clutched it with her hands as though for warmth or comfort. She looked physically ill.

I sat in a chair near her bedside, watching her for a few minutes, wondering what she was dreaming about. I had been exposed to Imperium Luminis in a relatively small dose, and from the beginning I was convinced that it was an illegitimate organization—but even I sometimes thought of Giuseppe Conti or Restoration House and believed, for an instant, that Imperium Luminis was, or could be, a force for justice and good. And if *I* could not fully dismiss such thoughts, then how confused must *Anna* be after months of full-scale indoctrination and sacrifice? When she joined Imperium Luminis she had traded one addiction for another; this process of reentering the real world must have been for her a delayed withdrawal.

"Anna," I said. "Anna."

She woke with a violent startle. When she saw me she smiled slightly and closed her eyes, succumbing to a yawn.

"I love you," I said. "And I'm sorry. Do you understand why I helped your stepfather?"

She got up and walked to the window. The day was bright and warm, the dune grass waving in a strong offshore breeze.

"I understand," she said. "I have a confession to make. All along I was trying to recruit you as a member of the Light."

"I know."

"But I did it for the same reasons that you were trying to get me away from them. I believed"—here she paused, evidently uncertain about her use of tense—"I believed that I had found the best way to live, that God's truth had been revealed to me. Imperium Luminis had saved me from my screwed-up life and for once I was *happy*. I only wanted to share it all with you. Every member of Imperium Luminis is expected to always be looking to bring the Light to others, to bring in new members. Of course I thought of you."

"We wanted to be together but we were working at it from opposite directions."

"Didn't you think it was a little odd that I came to visit you so soon after the note arrived from my stepfather?"

"Wait a minute. What are you saying?"

"I was already a member of the Light when I showed up in the rain at your apartment that day. And the note from Carl was fake—just something to get you to begin thinking about me."

I was floored, seized once again by anger and embarrassment at my gullibility. So the setup had gone back that far. Not only had Imperium Luminis lied about my father, but they had coerced Anna into playacting as well, all with a view to saving my soul. It was almost flattering, in a grotesque and manipulative way.

"What about when we slept together?" I said. "Was that part of the plan too?"

"No, that I did on my own."

She was silent, gazing out at the ocean. "Let's go down to the beach."

I imagined for a moment that Anna intended to escape, that when she got to the beach she would run, perhaps toward a car sent by Imperium Luminis. My face must have betrayed my concern, because she said, "Don't worry. I wanted to get away at the beginning, but now I'm past that. I just want to get some fresh air."

At Blake's insistence, we took two bodyguards along for good measure, one walking about ten feet in front of us and the other an equal distance behind. The morning was glorious, the sea as blue as the flawless sky, the light glinting off the waves as though through a thousand diamonds. The sun warmed the skin while a wet, cooler breeze came across the water.

"I'm betraying them," she said. "They gave me a new life and now I want to reject them."

"They were the ones who betrayed you. They took you in because you were vulnerable. They didn't really want to help you. They just wanted a new member—someone with money and connections, to boot."

"How can you be so sure?"

We were walking along the beach, just above the line in the sand that marked the highest progression of the lapping waves. Anna was proceeding with slow and wandering strides. She was downcast, idly kicking at little pieces of driftwood and seaweed.

She said, "Father Harrington told me just the other day, 'Your faith will be tested, and very soon. It will be tested to the maximum extent. If you fail the test, if you reject the Light, you will be utterly lost.'"

"The problem is that Harrington managed to convince you that Imperium Luminis equals faith. But you can say no to Imperium Luminis and still be a good person, even a good Catholic. Maybe there's a way to compromise."

"That's like leaving the Marine Corps to take a job as a security guard. It just wouldn't be the same. As the Benefactor says, 'Half-measures will not suffice with God.' It's all or nothing."

We reached a jumbled outcrop of boulders that jutted into the water. We climbed over the briny rocks, some of which were bearded with anemones. Every puddle in those tide-exposed rocks was its own ecosystem, teeming with invertebrate life.

"Tell me the truth," she said. "After all that you've seen of Imperium Luminis, can you really tell me that you believe *nothing*? You think it's all about power and money?"

"I love the idea of Imperium Luminis. A vast network of believers giving away their incomes and signing over their lives, working to remake the world according to God's plan. But I think Imperium Luminis found you can't achieve that sort of thing without restricting freedom and manipulating people."

"If it's a lie, it's a beautiful one."

"I'll tell you about lies. During my Exercises they had someone come in to impersonate a priest. Father Linus was the old pastor at Saint Cecilia's, someone I trusted. They had an actor pretend to be Father Linus. They had this person tell me all sorts of crazy stories about my father."

"How do you know it wasn't actually Father Linus?"

"My mother told me afterward that he had a stroke. It couldn't have been him."

"But why would they have lied?"

"They must have interviewed my father and gotten only part of the story."

We looked out to the horizon for a while.

"What did they do during your Exercises?" I said.

"We spent a lot of time talking about my mother. Why we didn't get along. How horrible and alone I felt when she died that winter." Anna paused and, for the first time that day, began to speak with her usual animation. "I was so angry with her for the divorce. It was like she just decided on a whim to leave my father and shack up with this rich guy. Where did that come from? Why was she ruining my life? During the Exercises, Father Harrington told me that my anger with her would never be satisfied, that I would have to move beyond anger and reach forgiveness."

She turned to me and said, "I feel like if I leave Imperium Luminis I'm going to lose everything. I'll be back to where I was before, when I was so angry and I didn't know who I was. My life has been one big blur, but during these incredible few months everything has come into focus."

"Didn't Gregory Blake tell you about the brainwashing techniques they use during the Exercises? I don't think that's a legitimate way to bring things into focus."

She nodded. "Mr. Blake said they give you a drug during the Exercises. I didn't believe him. Then he gave me a bunch of pills and had me swallow them. He turned out the lights. 'See,' he said. 'Doesn't that reproduce the sensations you felt during the Exercises?' It did. It totally did. I felt like I was twisting and turning through the dark, like I was on the verge of finding some special and peaceful place. It was a trick of pharmacology. But does that mean it was wrong? That *everything* was wrong?"

Anna was looking at me with a desperate, searching expression. I wanted to have the answers for her. I wanted to allay every doubt that had ever troubled her mind.

"You joined Imperium Luminis looking for something," I said. "Why don't you look to *me*? Let me be enough."

I was aware that the bodyguards, stationed on either side of the rock, were looking at us, but I didn't care. I kissed her. She joined in the kiss, though with a disappointing lack of enthusiasm.

"Let's go back in," she said with a sigh. We walked toward the house, which was on a hill ahead of us, gleaming in the rising sun.

THAT AFTERNOON, Barrett found me and said that my mother was on the phone. I raced into his study and grabbed the receiver.

"It's time," she said. "Come home now."

When I told Anna what was happening she said, "I'm going with you."

Blake was not eager to let her go, but he had said just about everything he needed to say to her. Barrett summoned his driver for us.

The anti-Exercises were finished.

THIRTEEN

IT'S A LONG DRIVE from Montauk to Astoria, and by the time we reached the house the sun had set and my father was gone. As we pulled up to the house I saw that the living-room window was wide open. When I was younger and my mother's father had died, the family kept the window open all night.

"This is the old tradition from Ireland," my mother had explained to me then. "The open window lets the spirit leave the house."

The white curtains billowed in the wind, which struck me as an ominous sight. It seemed that the house had been abandoned to the elements.

Anna and I entered the house and my mother rushed toward us from the kitchen. She embraced me, opened her second arm and clutched Anna to herself as well. There were voices in the kitchen and the smell of brewing coffee was strong in the air.

My mother brought Anna into the kitchen, where she was introduced to the neighbors as my girlfriend. I walked into the dining room alone. He was much as I had left him two days before, lying inert in the hospital bed. A clean white sheet had been laid over his body up to the neck. His expression was one of stoic dignity, a steeling of purpose to endure an unpleasant task. I was struck by the horrible stillness of the body, the silence of the room. Several candles were burning on the nearby table. A small crucifix had been brought in and propped against the wall. The breeze from the open window agitated the flames of the candles. The clock on the wall had been stopped at the hour of death. All of these details I remembered from my grandfather's wake; all were customs the family had brought over from Ireland, and they comforted me in a way I could not have anticipated—the thought that the same things were being done for my father as had been done for his father, and his father's father.

In the kitchen the women were talking.

"You're the one in Imperium Luminis, right?" Sue Donovan said.

Anna hesitated before saying, "Well, not anymore."

My mother joined me in the dining room.

"He just went," she said. "His breathing became more and more shallow. It was peaceful."

She put her hand to his cheek.

"My honey," she said, looking at him, her lips tensed and trembling. "I miss you already."

A gust of wind blew the curtains in response.

WE WAITED IN the kitchen until the man from the funeral parlor arrived. At one point Mrs. O'Brien from next door said, matter-of-factly, "Well, he's been called home. He's with God now."

Everyone murmured in assent. Anna and I looked at each other and, I could tell by her expression, shared a thought: could it really be that simple? Had we spent all this time tormenting ourselves and each other, when, in the end, the answer we were both looking for was to be found in the straightforward pronouncements of the next-door neighbor? He's been called home. This time on earth is a journey, a pilgrimage, and then we can come home, where all will be explained and forgiven.

The funeral director arrived and the body was taken out into an unmarked white van.

"I'm sorry for your loss," he said professionally. He was speaking to me specifically, as the only adult male present and presumably the person in charge. "Come by tomorrow around noon and we can discuss the particulars."

That was it for the night. The windows were to remain open and the candles were left to burn unattended. It occurred to me that this might result in the house burning down, but who could worry about a fire hazard when folk tradition dictated otherwise? The neighbors departed. My mother, on the advice of one of her friends, took a sleeping pill and retired. Anna and I went upstairs to my old room. In the dark, as we whispered in bed, I was surprised to feel moisture on Anna's cheeks.

"It's not fair," she said. "It's just not *fair.*"

She seemed to be speaking not just about the brain tumor, but also about her mother, and about leaving Imperium Luminis, and everything in general. I was unspeakably grateful that she was there with me.

She ran her hand under my shirt. She climbed on top of me and kissed me—tenderly at first, but with increasing purpose. I began to caress her body, those generous, soft curves I knew so well. I did not suppress my desire. I was surprised and almost disturbed by my ability to focus on her and her body at such a time. *This must be sacrilege,* I thought as she whipped her sweater off and tossed it aside in a single rapid motion. As we removed more clothing and began to touch each other without impediment, I realized that we were undertaking something new and different. We moved in the dark, progressing slowly and without the usual theatrics. The purpose was not to reach a passionate release, but to hold each other close enough that it would feel like we would never be apart.

Later, I was awakened by the sound of rain drumming on the window. For a few minutes I listened to the rain and felt Anna's warm, rhythmic breath on my neck. I got up and looked out the window. The rain was falling steadily. The arrival of raindrops in puddles was causing the reflections of the streetlamps to dance and waver. Every so often a car would proceed down the street, its wheels on the wet pavement sounding a gentle wissshhhhh. I remembered that the downstairs windows were wide open.

I walked through the dark, silent house. In the dining room the candles were burning, all of them having sent a quantity of molten wax cascading down their sides and onto the table. Their light flickered across the room, casting fantastic shadows on the walls. The hospital bed was empty. The sills and the floor beneath the windows were shiny and wet with the rain. I found a rag in the kitchen and mopped up the water.

I decided to leave the windows open. I found more rags and spread them on the windowsills and the floor to catch any additional rain.

Considering my handiwork, I wondered whether it would be sufficient to protect against the elements. I felt a surprising and overwhelming sense of comfort and peace, as if my father were there in the room with me, placing his large paw of a hand on my shoulder. For months, everything in my life had been tending toward disaster and disappointment. My father was dying. Anna was at the mercy of Imperium Luminis. Now, surrounded by the wavering glow of the candles, I thought that the worst was over. My father's suffering was over. Anna and I would be together. Events were no longer racing out of control. Everything was moving toward a conclusion—and I felt certain, for some reason, that the outcome would be acceptable, that the emptiness would not last.

WHEN MY MOTHER and Anna and I arrived at the funeral home for the wake, there was no one in the designated room—only the embalmed body in the corner. I had a terrible fear that not many people would come. My father was an only child from an extended family that specialized in only children, so there would be almost no one from his side in attendance. My mother's relatives would turn out, as would some co-workers from the Transit Authority. Aside from those people, however, I could not imagine who else would come to pay their respects. I recalled Maria Barrett's funeral, with the magnificent church of Saint Ignatius Loyola packed to the rafters as for a departed head of state. It seemed a harsh judgment that my father's day of memory would be so paltry in comparison.

I was amazed, less than an hour later, to be in the midst of a full house. Perhaps a hundred people were stuffed into the small room, and a retractable wall was removed to accommodate the crowd. The majority of these mourners came from Saint Cecilia's. My father had been involved in so many projects and committees at the church over the years that he seemed to have known every Catholic within several square miles. The level of conversation had begun low, out of respect, but as more people arrived and formed small conclaves, gossiping and chortling, the volume grew until the mood of the place changed from one of hushed memory to that of a successful party.

My mother and I stood near the coffin while the visitors filed past. Most people said something simple like, "I'm sorry for your loss," but there were also many who paused to give more personal testimony.

"We painted the steeple of the church together."

"He lent me five hundred bucks when I was between jobs."

"Jack kept an eye on my son after my husband died."

"He mowed my lawn when Patricia was ill last year."

One man, whom I did not recognize, embraced me and called me by my name. He was thickly bearded, dressed in old jeans and a faded polo shirt, and he smelled of stale cigarette smoke.

"I really loved that old bastard," he said. "When I heard the news, I just had to drive up here. Took all night."

My mother saw my embarrassed confusion and said, "You remember Peter Weathers."

"Christ, I haven't seen you since you were like this," he said, holding his palm a few feet above the floor and chuckling.

After he walked away, my mother whispered, "He's had a . . . difficult life."

I remembered him—Peter Weathers, who was a ghostly presence in my father's life. Every six months or so the phone would ring and it would be Peter Weathers. My father would lock the bedroom door to speak to him in privacy and emerge an hour later in a fantastically bad mood. As I got older I began to piece together the story. Peter Weathers was an old friend from the army who had not done well for himself after the war. He had drifted from job to job, living hand-to-mouth, at one point becoming involved in a car-theft scheme and spending time in jail.

I watched Peter Weathers for a few minutes, and when he headed for the door I followed him. I found him sitting on the railing of the small porch outside the funeral home, smoking a cigarette.

"Want one?" he said, gesturing with the pack. I said no.

"My father never really talked about the war."

"What would he have said?"

I decided to take a chance, if only to discover whether the stories from the Exercises were wholly fictional:

"He did tell me a little bit of one story, though. About when you were ambushed. And how the Vietcong killed everyone in a village that was nearby?"

"Yeah, that happened pretty much that way."

Peter Weathers took a long drag on his cigarette.

"'Course, that's leaving out quite a bit."

He gave me a sidelong look, as if to ask whether I wanted to hear the rest. I nodded.

"The reason we were in the area in the first place was there were reports of a large cache of weapons that the enemy was keeping in a certain village. We were supposed to go out there, find the weapons and blow the cache up. Problem was, when we got there and figured out the lay of the land, the weapons were next to a hospital. Next to a fuckin' hospital, can you believe it? We had a big debate about what to do, whether we should just finish the mission despite the hospital and let the souls of the dead be on the consciences of the barbarians who hid that stuff there, or whether we should tip off the villagers to what we were doing and potentially expose ourselves to harm."

He was speaking almost too quickly, tripping over the words in his eagerness to tell the full story. He paused and let a slow, strange smile spread across his lips.

"What would you have done?" he said.

"I don't know."

"Guess what your father wanted to do."

I didn't hesitate, and I took a certain joy in my confidence: "He wanted to tell them."

"You bet. We thought he was crazy, but he was insistent—and actually very persuasive. He said he was in Vietnam to defend his country, not to become a war criminal."

"So did you tell them?"

"We compromised. We moved into position around the hospital and then your father went in and told them they had ten minutes to clear out. Thinking back on it, it was such a stupid thing to do. There could have been thousands of Vietcong in the area, and we just marched in there like morons and asked permission to blow up their building. They could have shot your father on sight. Anyway, miracle of miracles, it all went according to plan. The hospital workers cleared out the patients, we set the charges and BOOM, the motherfucker went up like a fireworks factory."

Peter Weathers simulated the explosion with a sudden flailing of his hands.

"It was what happened next that we didn't anticipate. The enemy came to the conclusion that the villagers must have been collaborating with us—otherwise, how to explain the fact that they all got out of the area before we blew it up? It has a terrible logic to it, doesn't it? So they killed everyone they could find in the village, to make an example of them. Then they went after us. Then finally we went after them. And that's all she wrote."

I nodded to myself, pleased that my father had not been one of the advocates for destroying the hospital without warning. Peter Weathers must have noticed my smug approval, because he said, "You think your old man made the right decision?"

"Well, yes."

He jumped off the railing and moved his body close to mine, aggressively, intimately.

"Then tell that to the wife of Tommy Ventura. He was killed on our way out of the area. Shot right through the throat. As he died he was trying to breathe through the bullet hole. If we hadn't unzipped our fly and told them we were hanging around the neighborhood, we probably would have gotten away with no casualties. And the rest of the villagers would have been spared, too. You think your father ever forgot that, even for one minute of his fucking life?"

He stared at me with a crazed look, clearly contemptuous of what he took to be an absurd and blasphemous idea. He returned the cigarette to his mouth for another drag and exhaled, letting the wind catch hold of the smoke.

"Your father was one of the good guys," he said, shaking his head. "It all just tore him up. That day in particular. We went after those bastards and we killed every last one of them. And your father did it, but the whole thing just tore him up inside."

"Is that why he used drugs?"

"Hey, we *all* did the stuff. It was all over the place, like candy. And who has the right to judge that?"

"I'm just trying to understand."

"I was always happy for him, the way things turned out for him after he got home. He was able to make a go of it. He was trying to help me out, too, telling me to go to this rehab program, go talk to that doctor, or hey there's this job in the Bronx I know about from a friend . . ."

Peter Weathers threw his cigarette to the ground and stepped on it. We went back into the funeral home.

"He was real goddamned proud of you," he said. "Whenever I talked to him, he never would shut up about you."

I was supposed to be selecting pallbearers, so I asked Peter Weathers if he would do it. He seemed taken aback. The thought of carrying my father into the church and to the gravesite appeared to make the sense of loss more permanent to him. I wondered what memories of war or peace were causing him to stare confusedly at the carpet.

"You sure he would have wanted me?"

I said I was sure.

SAINT CECILIA'S IS an old church, built at the turn of the century with the dollars of immigrant parishioners who wanted a church reminiscent of the cathedrals and cavernous apses where they had worshipped in Europe. As we waited for the service to begin, I looked around the place—the dark wood latticework of the ceiling, the multi-colored stained-glass windows muted by the overcast day, the banks of candles glimmering along the shadowy side aisles. It had been many years since I had been inside Saint Cecilia's, and I found it oddly comfortable. I remembered receiving my first communion at the stone altar as a pious and trusting child. How strange to have rejected that communion, to have abandoned what my father believed, to have dragged Anna away from Imperium Luminis, and yet still to be able to sit in the pews of Saint Cecilia's and be soothed by the familiar surroundings, by the soaring strains of "Ave Maria" that were drifting down from the choir loft.

It was true, I thought. What they had told me about my father in the Exercises was true after all. And what my mother had told me about his heroin use was also true. Every revelation was a step closer to the truth. He was not simply, wholly and completely my boring old father. Having obtained the barest glimpse into his hidden self, I had discovered that he was also a professional killer, a war hero, a drug addict, a onetime psychiatric patient. I wanted to thank my father, to cheer for him, to celebrate his postwar life as an achievement that I had never suspected. But I also felt angry with him for almost depriving me of this knowledge. Was I not worthy of knowing these things?

I had declined to give a eulogy. My mind was a riot of memories and regret and anger and sadness, and had I taken the pulpit I would have been unable to synthesize any of this into an intelligible address.

The organ struck up the entrance hymn. We rose as one. The verses echoed in the dark chambers of the church: How precious did that grace appear, the hour I first believed.

My mother saw him first. She grabbed my arm and said, "Look." Anna turned around, trying to understand was what so remarkable about the sight of an elderly priest, robed in green and gold, shuffling up the center aisle to begin the funeral mass.

"I don't believe it," I said to her. "That's Father Linus."

THERE WAS A reception at the house after the service and the burial. The crowd was boisterous and loud. Drink flowed freely. I found Father Linus and took him aside.

"My mother said you had a stroke," I said. I noticed that the right side of his face drooped slightly, a downturning of the mouth and eye where the understructure of the skin had atrophied.

"Doctors are idiots and they don't know anything. A year ago they said I would never walk or speak normally again, and now they say that the brain has the capacity to adapt and recover. The truth is it's all in God's hands."

"I need to ask you something. Did you know my father was addicted to heroin after the war?"

He nodded. "He didn't want me to tell you. He was ashamed of the drugs right up until the end."

There was one remaining question that I could not answer, and I asked it less because I thought Father Linus knew the answer than out of a sense of general frustration.

"Why didn't he tell me anything until it was too late for me to talk to him about it? Where is the logic in that?"

"Don't you see? This was his gift to you—to never burden you with his past. For you, he always said the sky was the limit. Saint Brendan's, Princeton, law school. He kept you protected from everything that happened to him."

"He was disappointed in me, though. Because I decided not to go to law school. And especially because I didn't believe in God the way he did."

"He came to talk to me once about that. He said he was worried that you were losing your faith. I reminded him that *he* had gone through the same process of rejecting the Church before embracing it again. I told him that you were undertaking a search—and that it was a good thing, too, because it's worthless to have faith if you've never had to struggle for it. That's why I wasn't surprised to hear from Imperium Luminis about you."

"I've decided I don't agree with them."

"So what? Forget about them! There are a thousand ways to reach God. I've become very ecumenical in my old age. I've been reading the Koran and the Bhagavad Gita and the poetry of Sufi mystics. It's all holy. There is God in everything. The important thing is to never stop searching for the answer, or at least to never lose faith that the answer is out there somewhere—because it is."

I thanked Father Linus and allowed him to be mobbed by the parishioners of Saint Cecilia's who hadn't seen him since his illness and retirement. I found Anna standing alone on the back porch, sipping a glass of water.

"How are you doing?" she said.

I grabbed hold of her and gave her a bear hug, lifting her off the ground. She spilled her water on me.

"What's the matter with you?" she said.

"I know. I'm supposed to be sad right now, but for some reason I can't be."

I tried to explain how I was feeling but only ended up producing a stream of disjointed ideas—that the mysterious Father Linus in the Exercises had, in fact, been real; that my father had tried to save dozens of innocent lives in Vietnam, and that even if that meant he had sacrificed the lives of the villagers and some of his fellow soldiers, he had still done the right thing; that for the first time I was proud of him; that I wanted to tell him that I was proud, and somehow I felt that he already knew; that Anna and I would keep searching for the answers, together, and that *that* was the important thing.

"Are you drunk?" she finally said.

"Maybe a little."

"Listen, I want to talk to you about something."

There was a wariness in her tone that made me dread whatever she was about to tell me.

"I need to go talk to Father Harrington."

"Why? What for?"

"It's not right to just abandon Imperium Luminis without ever telling them, or at least thanking them for all they did for me. I owe them that much."

"I don't think you should go."

"You're worried they'll convince me to remain a member."

I nodded.

"I know what I want, and it's not the Light," she said. "It's you. It's always been you. Do you trust me?"

I nodded again.

"I want to go now, before I change my mind. I've figured out exactly what I want to say to Father Harrington. I already called my stepfather's driver. He's bringing the car to take me there, and afterward I'll come back here."

I walked her to the curb, where Barrett's black Mercedes was waiting. Just before she got into the back seat, some impulse moved me to grab her hand.

"Don't worry," she said. "I'll be back."

She kissed me and slipped into the back seat. The driver made a U-turn, and then the car sped off into the night.

FOURTEEN

I SPENT THAT NIGHT downstairs waiting for Anna to return. The place was a mess from the reception, the furniture displaced to strange locations. I did some cleaning, paged through a few magazines and dozed off on the sofa. In the morning I woke with a start, somehow having realized in my dream that the night was over and still Anna had not come back to me.

I told myself that she was just delayed, or that the hour had been too late and she had decided to return to her old apartment in the Aurelian. She would call soon and everything would be fine.

In the kitchen I rummaged through the cupboards and found a box of pancake mix. I put some coffee on. By the time my mother appeared, tying her old pink robe about herself, I had already produced a tall stack of pancakes and was moving on to fried eggs.

"What's all this?" she said.

"I don't think I've ever been so hungry," I said. "I don't know why."

I served her a large plate of food. She poured syrup over her pancakes and began to eat slowly. She looked drawn and tired. I guessed that she had not slept during the night and was now only mechanically going through the motions of the morning.

"You know what I was thinking last night?" she said after a long period of silence. "There are so many terrible people in the world, and people who don't have any family to miss them. I was thinking how unfair it is that they're here while your father is gone. I guess that's selfish."

The phone rang and my mother got to it first. I breathed a sigh of relief—it would be Anna. My mother rolled her eyes as she picked up the receiver, wondering who could be so rude as to call at sunrise the morning after her husband died.

"Yes, he's here," she said. Turning to me: "It's Carl Barrett."

IT WAS A HUMID, waterlogged day and the lights inside the triangles of the Transatlantic Building were sending a warm glow into the cloudy murk. I ascended to the top floor and was shown immediately into Carl Barrett's office.

"We've got a problem," Barrett said, indicating that I should sit in the chair in front of his desk.

"Where is she?"

"Did you know she was going back to talk to Harrington?"

"She felt she needed to explain why she was leaving. Where is she?"

"She had my driver bring her to the Imperium Luminis house in Greenwich Village. She went inside and never came out. The driver waited all night and finally gave up. He just reported all this to me a few hours ago."

I stared at the carpet for a moment, absorbing the impact of this new development. A vague terror arose within me. Had Anna been lying to me ever since we left Montauk, buying time until she could return to Imperium Luminis? I remembered her words as she left after the funeral: "*I know what I want, and it's not the Light. It's you. It's always been you. Do you trust me?*" I would have staked my life on her sincerity.

"She was totally committed to leaving Imperium Luminis," I said. "There's no way she was lying."

"Even so, you know how they operate. Did you really think they would just let her walk out of there? They probably put her into some sort of emergency Exercises or something." He shook his head and added, in a scolding tone, "It really wasn't very smart to let her go there, even temporarily."

He was right. I thought back to that moment when Anna was getting into the car. Why hadn't I done more to stop her? In the aftermath of the funeral, in the face of the bleak fact of my father's death, I had found in Anna my best and only reason for hope. I thought our troubles were over and we would live happily ever after. Could she really have been taken from me, and so quickly?

Barrett shook his head and said, "In my line of business you learn to accept the inevitable once it reveals itself. If you're beaten, you're beaten. How long can we keep this up?"

"No. It can't end this way. I'm going down there."

AT THE TOWNHOUSE in the village I demanded to see Father Harrington. The receptionist clearly disapproved of my tone, but she picked up the phone and said I was there to see the director. She showed me into his office. I remembered the room from my first visit to the Imperium Luminis house, just after Anna had joined the group. It seemed like a lifetime, or two or three, had passed since then.

Harrington was seated in an armchair reading a book. He was wearing a Roman collar, the first time I had seen him in his priestly garments. A dim lamp behind his head did little to illuminate the dark room.

"Well, well," he said, resting the book on his leg.

"I want to see Anna."

"And you think she's here?"

"I know she's here."

"Oh?" he said, feigning surprise. "How?"

"Carl Barrett told me his driver dropped her off here last night, and she never came out of the building."

With an open hand, Harrington invited me to sit in an armchair that was facing his. I did not move. I wanted to maintain my tone of righteous indignation, and accepting his offer of a seat would have conveyed the message that I was interested in a tranquil discussion. He remained silent. I understood that he would only speak once I was comfortably ensconced across from him. I hesitated, but complied.

"I must confess, I'm not sure how to deal with this situation," he said, as though considering an intractable question of philosophy. "You have done everything in your power to destroy the deep and abiding faith of this young girl. You have lied to us. You undertook the Exercises under false pretenses. You participated in a kidnapping. And you did it all for love, apparently. If only you could see that your idea of love is incomplete. If only you would devote yourself to the love of God with the same passion and energy with which you have pursued Anna."

"I didn't come here to talk about God. I want to see Anna, and I know she wants to see me."

"That may very well be the case. Unfortunately, she's not here. In fact, she didn't come here last night at all."

I made a sort of snorting sound to indicate my certainty that he was lying. My gaze did not waver from his eyes. Harrington sighed deeply and shook his head.

"Never let it be said that I'm not a sentimentalist," he said. "Believe it or not, I sympathize with you. I know you've just lost your father, and I'm deeply sorry. I can guess how important it must seem to be with Anna at a time like this. I'm going to tell you where she is, even though the far wiser course of action, given your history with us, would be to escort you off the premises."

He set his book aside and went to his desk. He opened his laptop computer and switched it on. It made a gentle chiming sound. The computer whirred as it recalled and processed whatever information was necessary for it to function. Harrington placed an unlabeled compact disc into the drive. He brought the laptop back to his seat and angled the computer so that I could see the screen.

"We've been following Anna ever since the two of you ventured onto the street outside Restoration House."

At the touch of a button, a photograph appeared on the screen. It was taken by the security camera atop the gate at Restoration House, and it showed Anna and me walking down the street in Riverdale. After a brief delay, the photo was replaced by another—two sedans and several men surrounding Anna, who was poised for struggle.

"Our people followed the car out to Montauk."

A picture of the posterior of a sedan on the Long Island Expressway.

"We monitored what was happening on the Barrett property while you were there. We followed you two back to Astoria. When Anna left your house last night, we followed her again."

More digital pictures flickered across the screen, demonstrating the scenes as he narrated. I was surprised to see a shot, through a telephoto lens, of the two of us standing on the rocks on the beach below the house in Montauk.

"Carl Barrett's car did not bring her here last night. It went out to Nassau County and stopped at a motel."

Another shot of a car on the Long Island Expressway. Anna getting out of a car in a motel parking lot.

"And here she is entering a room in the motel with the man who was driving the car."

I strained to see the picture closely, disbelieving what Harrington was saying. He passed the computer to me. Sure enough, the photo appeared to show Anna walking down the exterior walkway of a cheap motel toward an open door. The man behind her was following very closely, possibly directing her against her will. The expression on her face was grainy and therefore ambiguous—perhaps angry, perhaps resolute.

Were the pictures fake? And if they were legitimate, what on earth could they mean?

"You don't agree with our conservative philosophy, which is your prerogative. You think we restrict people's freedom, which is arguable. But that hardly makes us *evil*. If anything, we are benignly deluded. What if the real evil has been staring you in the face all along and you didn't see it? What do you know about Carl Barrett, anyway?"

"This isn't about him."

Harrington continued, lowering his voice almost to a whisper.

"Actually, it's entirely about him. You think of Carl Barrett as a harmless old man, a rich tycoon with a soft spot for his only stepdaughter. What if you're wrong? What if he's a ruthless businessman who sees her as a *liability*? He called us here a few weeks ago, accusing us of trying to blackmail him through Anna. He thinks we're after his money. He doesn't care about her happiness, or your happiness. He just wants to make sure Anna won't rejoin the Light. She already has a significant portion of his money in a trust fund that he can't reclaim. The last thing he wants is for us to get that money."

I was beginning to see where Harrington was going with this argument. It was a chain of logic that would explain the pictures he had shown me—if, of course, the pictures were real.

"Carl Barrett sees *you* as a liability," Harrington said. "After all, you were raised as a Catholic. You've spent time at Restoration House. In his eyes, you may be a member of the Light yourself, or at least sympathetic to us. You might convince her to come back to the Light. Don't you see? You served your purpose and stole her away from the Light, and now you're expendable. The solution is to take her away again, to let Gregory Blake continue his destructive work until every last shred of resistance is broken. He will poison her against us, and against you, too."

Harrington took the computer from my lap, where it had been idling, its screen filled with pulsating, shape-shifting bands of color. He called up several more pictures from the CD.

"You don't think Carl Barrett is capable of this? Remember, this is a man who associates with some of the shadiest characters in New York.

He used to get a personal Christmas card every year from John Gotti— even from prison. You still don't believe me? Here is a picture of another car pulling up at the motel. Here is Gregory Blake getting out of the car. Here he is entering Anna's motel room."

I searched the screen as closely as I could. I wanted to understand the image on the level of the individual pixels. Harrington removed the CD from the computer and threw the disc onto my lap.

"You've never even given us a chance," he said. "You've been biased against us from the beginning and, because you closed your mind, you've missed a chance for real happiness. We may have our quirks, even our flaws, but in the end Imperium Luminis is just an organization of good people trying to do the right thing in a complicated world. We're not the monsters you think we are. In fact, *we're* the good guys. Just remember, if you ever realize the mistake you've made, if you want to come back, we would forgive you. We've already forgiven you. We would welcome you with open arms."

Harrington lifted his hands from the arms of his chair and showed me his palms, demonstrating his invitation for a figurative embrace. I took the CD and walked toward the door. Just as I was about to exit the room, I said, almost without intending to, "Thank you, Father."

I PAUSED ON the corner down the block from the townhouse. I held the CD in my hand, turning it slightly so that a rainbow of light spiraled across the metal where the information was encoded.

Could Harrington be telling the truth? Pictures—especially digital ones—can be manipulated. Maybe Harrington had actually convinced Anna to return to Imperium Luminis. Maybe he was inventing an elaborate lie to prevent me from trying to find her and once again persuade her to leave the Light.

I put the CD away and thought: *I'll ask my father. He'll know what to do.*

But, of course, I instantly realized my slip; and I felt alone in a new and cruel way.

FIFTEEN

I EXAMINED the pictures carefully on our home computer. I blew them up to a hundred times their original size, at which point they disintegrated into abstract patterns of color. I had no idea what signs or markings would indicate that the photos had been tampered with. Certainly nothing looked obviously out of place—no shadows falling in impossible directions, no inconsistencies in tone or hue. There was the light source. How did the shadows creep around the sides of the objects? It all looked legitimate.

My mother was watching TV virtually around the clock. Her capacity for discrimination seemed to have vanished, so that she could now watch a second-rate talk show for the full hour to discover the shocking results of the paternity tests, whereas before she would have rolled her eyes in derision. She was also taken with police procedurals—the brutal crimes; the sullen, heroic detectives; the confessional psychodrama of the interrogation room. She did not seem to be enjoying these shows, however. She simply stared at the TV with a blank expression, clicking among the channels, looking for something better.

THAT NIGHT, past two in the morning, the phone rang. I threw the covers off and sprinted for the phone—not hoping, but somehow knowing, who was calling.

"Listen, I can't talk long," Anna said, whispering.

"Where are you?"

"I don't know. Some motel somewhere. I managed to steal Gregory Blake's cell phone from his jacket, but I only have a minute. They're right outside the door."

"Did you go to see Harrington last night?"

"I never got there. I told the driver to take me there but he called Gregory Blake, who apparently thought that I wanted to rejoin the Light. So he told the driver to bring me out here. Matt, this is getting out of control. Blake is telling me all sorts of crazy things."

"About me?"

"Some of it. You're not really a member of the Light, are you?"

"Don't believe anything he says."

"Why are they doing this?"

"Do you have a trust fund?"

"It matures in two years. Why?"

"Just hold on. I'm going to find you."

"Shit—here they come. I love you."

I MIGHT NOT have believed Father Harrington, but I *knew* Anna wasn't lying. I heard the truth and the confusion in her voice. She was scared, bewildered and terribly alone. I didn't sleep for the rest of the night. I imagined the scene: the dilapidated motel, the shabby bureau missing its topmost knobs, the lingering scent of old cigarette smoke, Gregory Blake quietly and persistently hectoring her—going beyond the restoration of free will, introducing to her mind ideas that were as false and hurtful as those espoused by Imperium Luminis. I waited with anguished anticipation for the day to begin.

When the sun finally appeared, I took the train into the city and presented myself to the receptionist at the Barrett Properties offices in the Transatlantic Building. I told her I had information about Carl Barrett's daughter and that it was a matter of great importance that I see him immediately. She said he was not in the office yet but was expected within the hour.

I took a seat to wait for him. I fingered the CD in my pocket, rehearsing the meeting in advance.

"Matt," Barrett said, striding into the office. "Come inside. Jesus, you look awful."

He removed his suit jacket and sat behind his desk. His shirt was a shade of pure, blinding white.

"What is it?" he said. "What's happened?"

"Your driver never took Anna to Imperium Luminis. They went to a motel on Long Island so that Gregory Blake could continue to work on her. But you already knew that, didn't you?"

Barrett adopted a look of boundless perplexity.

I produced the CD and, pointing to his computer, said, "May I?"

It was a flat-screen system, the very latest and sexiest computer that money could buy. On the screen ran an infinite scrolling ticker of financial information. I opened the CD drive and launched the application to display the evidence. The computer hesitated for a few seconds, as though stymied by the request, but it performed whatever conversions or corrections needed to be carried out. The first photograph, from the security camera at Restoration House, appeared on the screen.

"Imperium Luminis followed her," I said.

I narrated the timeline as the pictures scrolled past.

When I reached the final shot of Gregory Blake entering the motel room, Barrett said, "Don't tell me you believe them."

"Why shouldn't I?"

"Because they're manipulative, and dedicated to accumulating power and money by any means necessary."

"And how are *you* any different? You've been lying to the world about your past for years. Why should I believe *you*?"

Barrett stood suddenly and came around the desk toward me. I thought for a moment that he intended to throttle me, but when he spoke his tone was not menacing.

"I wouldn't have thought it in a million years," he said. "You're just as confused as Anna is. These people are absolutely masterful."

"And the pictures?"

"They're fake, of course. Anyone with a computer could put those together."

He was staring at me with a compassionate, paternal expression, and for a second I doubted myself. The pictures could be counterfeit. And Anna's phone call? It was impossible that she would lie to me of her own free will, but couldn't Imperium Luminis have been somehow *forcing* her to say those words?

"What about your driver?" I said. "I'd like to talk to him."

Barrett shook his head.

"He quit yesterday."

This was highly suspicious, although the driver's disappearance could have cast blame on either Imperium Luminis or Barrett—it all depended on the driver's primary affiliation. I was beginning to lose heart. Anna was either taken to a Nassau County motel at Carl Barrett's direction or the whole story was concocted by Imperium Luminis. And if Anna *was* with Imperium Luminis, either she was complicit in the lie or she was herself deceived. All possibilities were equally plausible. I could think of no way to reach the truth. It was essential that I see Anna. I had to choke back my sense of floundering panic lest I embarrass myself in front of Barrett. Everything—*everything*—depended on my future with Anna, and there seemed no possibility of finding her. I thought of her parting words to me. *I know what I want, and it's not the Light. It's you. It's always been you* . . .

"Please," I said. "If you know where she is, please just let me see her."

Barrett put his hands on my shoulders and squeezed hard.

"Pull yourself together," he said. "I don't have any idea where she is. All we can do is wait."

FOLLOWING THAT MEETING with Carl Barrett, not knowing who to believe or how to find Anna, I finally abandoned all logic. The one incontrovertible fact I could grasp was that Anna had been taken by *someone* to a motel in Nassau County. I borrowed my parents' old Chevy and took a long, aimless drive around Long Island. I printed out the picture of the motel from the CD that Harrington had given me. I searched the highways of Nassau County for the site. There were hundreds of motels in the county—which, when you think about it, is not such bad odds if you give yourself enough time to check them all out. I drove in a sort of daze, lost in thoughts about Anna and my father. I came to attention after many miles had passed on the odometer and wondered how I had been driving during the elapsed time. My only company was the radio. As I drove, the stations would fade, the frequencies interfering and crackling and finally resolving into melancholy ballads or the jaunty harmonizing of boy bands.

On the way out to Long Island I passed the Kosciuszko Bridge and looked out over the vast cemetery where my father was buried. I did not think of visiting the gravesite. The earth was still scarred and there would be no headstone for a few more weeks. It was a quintessential New York cemetery, with smokestacks in the near distance and the gravestones crowded together—cross to cross—like commuters on the subway. All those anonymous dead, piling on top of one another! It would have been more agreeable to have buried my father in a bucolic spot where the leaves would change and the sea would surge. I thought of Truro or Montauk. But, of course, that close New York spot suited him best.

I did not manage to locate the motel from the picture.

I returned home, exhausted and dispirited, to find a black Mercedes at the curb of my parents' house.

"Matthew Kelly?" the unfamiliar driver said. "Carl Barrett would like to see you right away."

He held the door open and I climbed inside.

THE CAR TOOK me toward the waterfront of Queens. It was a land-scape of factories and warehouses that was lonely and grimy during the day; now, well into the evening, it was utterly deserted. As we continued toward the river, the neighborhood became even more disreputable, populated mostly by abandoned assembly plants and rusting machinery guarded by dogs. The fantastical thought occurred to me that the rumors of Mafia ties were true, that Barrett was having me brought there for the same reasons that mobsters used to drive people to the Meadowlands in New Jersey—solitude and a dearth of witnesses.

"Where are we going?" I said to the driver, who replied, cryptically, "The place by the river."

He was not lying. At length we came within sight of a chain-link fence that supported a small white sign: BARRETT PROPERTIES. We passed through a gate and rolled to a stop. The ground was neither dirt nor pavement, but a kind of man-made soil created by the decay prod-ucts of ancient asphalt. There were crumbling wharves nearby, and the wide face of a large, ruined factory facing the river. The derelict citi-zenry of the neighborhood had made the building into a canvas, scrawl-ing indecipherable messages and names on its walls. After taking a moment to survey these surroundings, I spotted a white-haired figure in an overcoat standing at a railing near one of the docks. As I approached, Carl Barrett turned to me and said, "Imagine what this was going to become."

He gestured to the dark factory and the darker air above it.

"I was thinking of calling it Barrett City, but I wasn't sure. I'm enough of an egomaniac to consider such an idea but probably not enough of one to go through with it. In case you haven't noticed, there is virtually nowhere left to build anything on a grand scale in Manhattan. But here, only a few hundred yards away, just across the river, are acres and acres of land lying unused. I bought this property and the ones to the north and the south. I was going to build a luxury apartment complex here, a new outpost of Manhattan, three gleaming towers of light. And here is the beautiful part—a twenty-four-hour-a-day ferry across the river, right to the heart of midtown in ninety-seven seconds."

He paused and took in the sweeping, vertiginous view of the skyline.

"The Transatlantic Building was big, but this was going to be bigger."

I didn't know what he wanted me to say. I doubted he had brought me out there to pitch ideas for real estate ventures. I was concerned by his choice of verb tense, as well as by his generally elegiac tone.

"I was summoned to the Imperium Luminis house for a meeting with Father Harrington," he said.

"Did he say where Anna is?"

"First things first. He asked me for a donation again. He began to tell me all about the wonderful things Imperium Luminis could do with the money. Not that there was ever any mention of a quid pro quo, no 'You give us this donation and we give you your daughter back.' Nothing that explicit. But that was clearly what he was suggesting."

"Please tell me you agreed to give him the money. Isn't it worth it at this point?"

"Agreed to give him the money? He was asking for nine figures! I'm fortunate enough to be wealthy, but that's too much even for me to part with. I told him he could go fuck himself. I told him I'd had enough of Imperium Luminis. I told him I was ready to use all my influence and call in all my political favors to force the district attorney to charge him with kidnapping. I gave him a piece of my mind, all right. When I was finished, he just smiled and handed me a piece of paper."

He stopped and looked at me as though *I* should know what was on the paper. The location of Anna's confinement? The secret name of the Benefactor? The formula that would reduce everything that had occurred and everything that was going to occur into one terrifying and sublime equation?

"What was on the paper?" I said.

"You really don't know? I wasn't sure whether you were in on it."

Barrett turned to me, his lower jaw quivering, his eyes incandescent with fury. I thought he was going to hit me, and I weighed whether or not I should defend myself. He thrust his face close to mine and said, in a voice drained of all its affected civility, a voice in the cadence of a poor, frustrated Brooklyn boy born unfairly below his proper station, "You stupid fucking . . . *mick*. I was right about you from the beginning. I always thought that somehow, some way, you would fuck up Anna's life, but I was wrong. It's *my* life you fucked up."

"I don't understand."

He regained his composure and withdrew a few feet. He adopted an ironical smile.

"The paper contained details of financial transactions carried out by my company. In particular, deposits to various offshore bank accounts that, with some elementary investigation, could be tied to members of the city council and the zoning commission."

"Bribes?"

"To someone who doesn't understand my business and the way deals are made in the real world, yes, 'bribes.' How do you think a place like this is rezoned from industrial to residential? Because I ask them politely? Harrington said that no one in the media had seen the information, but that he could not guarantee its continued secrecy. Then he repeated his request for a donation."

"What does this have to do with me? I had nothing to do with this."

Barrett shook his head, as though he understood and sympathized with my bewilderment.

"It was the *photographs*. The photographs you loaded onto my computer. It took the security people at my office quite a while to figure out what had happened. When you put the CD into the computer, it loaded a program onto the hard drive that began to record all the keystrokes I typed. It sent that information, disguised as an e-mail, to Imperium Luminis. One of the keystroke combinations was my password to what my computer people had assured me was an impenetrable network. They said this was the work of a master programmer, someone who knew how to access and manipulate the source code of the operating system. All Imperium Luminis had to do was log in and look around for anything incriminating."

I stared at him for some time before finally saying, "Oh my God." The whole scheme began to become clear. Doctor some photographs. Dupe the lovestruck and distraught protagonist. And what about Anna's phone call? Was *she* in on the conspiracy?

"Of course this is enough to put me in prison for a year or two," Barrett said. "The deal that Imperium Luminis proposed is really very reasonable. I turn over about three-quarters of my net worth, as well as the majority of shares in the company, to Imperium Luminis. In turn, they keep the information under wraps. As a guarantee that they won't demand additional payments in the future, I'm going to move to Switzerland, where I will be immune from any legal charges. I'll keep more than enough money to live a comfortable lifestyle. Suddenly, I'm retired. It all ends here. The whole incredible, horrible journey."

I wondered about his journey, what sacrifices it took for him to reach the top—what moral circumventions, what unpalatable associations, what truces with his conscience.

He turned his back to me and faced the skyline of midtown. Directly across from us was the Empire State Building, and farther uptown glowed the dispassionate triangles of the Transatlantic Building, hovering and slowly changing color above the fervent city. I tried to guess at the unseen expression on Carl Barrett's face. As stunned as I felt about being an unwitting participant in his relative ruination, I could not quite bring myself to feel sorry for him. If he had sought greatness and success, he had achieved it. If he deserved punishment for his history of vague misdeeds and apparent corruption, it had now been meted out. He would prosper in retirement, I knew—barreling down alpine ski slopes, shuttling from the opera house to his villa on the lake. People like Carl Barrett would always come out all right. The world, after all, was made for him.

Only one question remained, only one.

"What about Anna?"

"Harrington wouldn't tell me. He wants to talk to you."

SIXTEEN

BEFORE YOU SAY a word—"

Father Harrington stood and approached me, putting his index finger to his lips to silence me. As he came closer, it appeared that he wished to shake my hand, a prospect that I found repugnant. He continued toward me, however, until he stood only a foot or so from my body. It seemed that he was going to hug me. I jumped backward, astonished at this strange gesture.

But he did not embrace me. He asked me to untuck my shirt. Just as I was beginning to suspect some even greater impropriety, I realized that he was simply checking to make sure I was not wearing a wire. I showed him the skin of my chest and back. He patted my legs, as a policeman looks for a weapon. Satisfied, he sat down behind his desk and said, "What can I do for you?"

"You've ruined my life. Do you know that?"

"We haven't ruined anything. It was *you* who rejected the Light."

"The Light! The Light is just a criminal enterprise and you're a con man. Blackmailing Carl Barrett? Lying to me? How does it all square with what Christ would have done? The ends don't justify the means."

"Where did you learn that?" he said. "In kindergarten?"

Harrington chuckled and leaned toward me.

"We were not put here to dawdle," he said. "We will be called to account for our failures to act on God's will. As the Benefactor says, 'Half-measures will not suffice.' And should we say in our defense, 'I didn't want to offend such-and-such person,' or 'I didn't want to break that law,' or 'I was too fainthearted to correct that injustice,' we will have failed. *We must then become His means.*"

"You can't make the world a perfect place."

"Is that a reason to do nothing?"

"But you're doing more harm than good."

"And what exactly is the harm in the case that we're discussing now? Carl Barrett is a fraud, a criminal and a thoroughly corrupt man. Under our new arrangement, his fortune will help the poor around the world. We're starting new medical missions and AIDS treatment centers in Zimbabwe and Ukraine. We're expanding the Restoration House model to Los Angeles and Miami and Boston. Carl Barrett, meanwhile, still gets to retire in relative luxury. Do you really think God would be unhappy with this arrangement?"

I felt trapped by these specifics in a losing debate.

"But it's wrong," I said lamely. "It's wrong to steal and lie."

"Let me tell you a story. In the early days of Imperium Luminis, just as the Benefactor was beginning to spread his message, he began to hear strange things about what was happening to the Jews in northern Italy. It appeared that they were being deported to Germany for purposes and fates unknown. The Benefactor understood what was happening. He secured an abandoned monastery in the most remote corner of Sicily, on the very edge of Europe, and he began to shelter Jewish refugees there. They came one or two or three at a time, often smuggled by sea out of Trieste or Genoa. By the end of the war there were more than six hundred residents of this old monastery—all Jews, all otherwise fated to die."

"This isn't in *The Pilgrim*."

"Of course not. He wrote that book during the course of the war. He couldn't very well let Mussolini know what he was up to in Sicily. The point is that the Benefactor understood God's will. He was willing to go against what his society required, to risk everything for the defense of what is right. He did not blink at injustice, but set about trying to banish it from the world."

"Very nice," I said, not quite seeing where Harrington was going with this.

"I'll tell you what," he said. "If you can convince me that there is a difference between what the Benefactor did and what we have done with Carl Barrett, I'll give the money back and apologize to him."

I was in no mood to play these games of philosophical justification. If Harrington wanted to claim he knew the will of God, if he wanted to drag the rest of the world into accordance with the plan of the Almighty, then what *wouldn't* be permitted? It was a matter best resolved by theologians and terrorists. There was only one question I cared about answering.

"Just tell me one thing," I said. "What did Anna know?"

Harrington nodded and said, "Yes, I can see how that would be important to you." He paused and seemed to weigh the consequences of revealing the truth about her role. Finally he sighed and said, "She didn't know anything. We ordered her to help us put Carl Barrett's money to better use, but she refused to do anything more than ask him to make some donations. In fact, when we pushed her for more, she almost left the Light. We were very disappointed in her. But it was still too early in her training for her to understand, so we decided to use . . . another strategy. We didn't want to lose her. She has the gift of strong faith in God and the Benefactor."

I could think of yet another reason they didn't want to lose her—at least not before her trust fund matured.

"I don't suppose you'll ever let me see her?"

Harrington shrugged his shoulders.

"It's up to you," he said. "There is only one way for that to happen, and that would be for you to join the Light—for real this time. After what happened at Restoration House, we would expect you to work hard and remain faithful for a long, long time before we would trust you to see Anna. But nothing is impossible. All you have to do is truly accept the Light."

Harrington stared at me with a soothing, sympathetic gaze.

"You have wanted to believe all along," he said. "When your father was dying, when you were undertaking the Exercises. You have a deep desire for the love and peace of God's presence. Why are you fighting it?"

He came around to the front of the desk and put his hand on my shoulder.

"This is the fundamental question you have to answer for yourself: now that your father is dead, has he utterly disappeared or has he been called home to the greater life? I can assure you that his death is not meaningless. God has been watching you and seeking to comfort you all along. Why reject Him?"

"Don't you dare bring up my father."

"Your father wanted you to join the Light. He said this to Anna when she visited him in the hospital. Here is the life that God wants for you: two or three years from now, you and Anna, married, happy, living in some beautiful place—maybe even Sicily—and performing great acts of love and mercy. We also run schools in Chicago and Milwaukee and Oakland and Seattle. Perhaps you would like to teach in one of them. You have a chance at achieving a perfect life with Anna. If you reject the Light, where will you go? Matt, where will you go?"

I did not know the answer to his question. An impossible riddle seemed to knot together all the ragged threads of my life: after everything that had happened, could I really bring myself to join the Light—even if only to reach Anna? Conversely, could I give her up to be free?

"I don't know what to do," I said.

"Don't worry. Think it over. Look deep within yourself. The answer will come to you."

I left Harrington's office and did not look back. The world seemed to reel before me as I headed for the street.

It was then, as I staggered down the hallway with my mind in utter confusion, that I saw Gregory Blake. He was sitting comfortably in the parlor, reading *The New York Times*. I arrested my escape and stared at him for a second, to make sure it truly was him.

"What are *you* doing here?" I said. "Don't tell me you rejoined the Light?"

He looked up from his paper and watched me. He seemed to be waiting for me to say something else, or understand something.

"You never left the Light, did you?" I whispered. "You were with Imperium Luminis all along."

He smiled and turned back to his newspaper.

GOING HOME, I rode in the front car of the subway. In a state of bewildered awe, beyond resentment or anger, I marveled at the intricacy and skill of the Empire of Light. I'd had no idea what I was up against. How far back did the conspiracy go? What in my life had been due to chance and what had been orchestrated by them? Anna showing up at my apartment, pretending to be lost and directionless when in fact she was already working for the Light. The introduction of Gregory Blake, the counterfeit adversary, who would pretend to despise the Light in order to advance the plan. Everything had been masterfully organized to get the better of Carl Barrett.

I wondered whether I could trust Harrington when he said that Anna did not know the ultimate purpose of the plan. Wasn't that, after all, exactly what I wanted to hear? When Anna was sealed up in that bedroom on Montauk with Gregory Blake, were they *both* acting, following a script for my benefit? Or was Blake purposely putting Anna through a legitimate crisis of faith? I remembered a passage from *The Pilgrim*. As Giuseppe Conti was beginning to gather the people and resources to found Imperium Luminis, he wondered who would make the best members:

Blessed are they who have been put to the test—who are confronted with doubts and questions and who all but lose heart. If they endure and maintain their faith, they will be more perfect for their trial, hardened by the harsh fire of skepticism. Such, I thought, would be the ideal candidate for this new organization that was fast becoming my life's work.

I understood that Anna had to be innocent of the larger scheme. She had agreed to recruit me to the Light, but that was as far as her involvement went. Just as Giuseppe Conti prescribed in *The Pilgrim*, Gregory Blake had been putting her to the test to see if she would remain true to the Light. Her distress out on Montauk was too extreme to have been false. She had cried in my arms like a lost child on the night of my father's death. No one could fake that kind of distress. To me, her suffering was a proof of her sincerity. I couldn't *not* believe in her. Belief in Anna seemed to be hard-wired into my soul.

The only question was how and under what circumstances I could be with her.

I stood and walked to the front window of the subway car. The anonymous motorman was beside me, sealed up in his small cab. We careened through the endless dark tunnels at close to maximum speed. Signals flew past us. Signs marking switches floated into the narrow zone of illumination from our headlights and then vanished.

I remembered one day, long ago, when I accompanied my father on one of his runs. He kept the door to the motorman's cab open so that I could stand next to him and watch him working the controls. I was only about six years old at the time, and the sight of my father operating the great, shuddering machine made a tremendous impression on me. It seemed as wonderful a vocation as driving a fire truck or piloting a fighter plane.

That run was on the 7 line, in one of the old redbirds. At one point we came to a stop at a red signal outside the 69th Street station. It was the morning rush, and the trains were stacked up all the way into Times

Square. It was a slow run of starts and stops, the equivalent of a traffic jam. My father and I watched the people on the platform a hundred feet ahead of us. The tracks were elevated there, and by then the sun had risen, the morning in full force. A man in a suit checked his watch and glared at us, driven to frustration by the sight of the train parked just outside the station.

My father turned to me and said, " '*Crowds of men and women attired in the usual costumes, how curious you are to me!*' That's Walt Whitman, Matt."

In my childish ignorance, I thought my father meant that the impatient man on the platform was known to him and named Walt Whitman. It was only later that I learned that Walt Whitman was a poet, and the subject of my father's honors thesis at Columbia; and it was even later that I learned that most subway motormen—indeed most people in general—do not quote him from memory.

AT HOME, I found my mother asleep on the couch. Our collection of photo albums was spread out on the coffee table and seemed to have exploded. Hundreds of pictures had been freed from their plastic sleeves and were scattered in loose piles. On one side of the table was a new album. I opened it and found a chronological arrangement of pictures of my father. My mother had made a scrapbook of his life.

So, here he was as a plump baby, staring out from his crib. Here he was as a boy from the neighborhood with a crew cut and a stickball bat in his hand. And as a college student, at a party with my young mother, looking at once sheepish and exhilarated by their love. And here he was as a new father, dangling me from his arms, wearing the uniform of the Metropolitan Transit Authority.

But something was missing in the chronology she had constructed. I rummaged through the pictures on the table until I found the one I was looking for, the one I had kept for so long in my bureau drawer—the only picture I had ever seen of my father in Vietnam. The olive uniform, the sleeves rolled up past his elbows, the background of the dusty truck. The greenish tint over everything in the faded picture. My father's ambiguous smile.

I put that picture into the new scrapbook, just before the photo of him and his newborn baby. I thought it looked proper and complete. I wondered about the other events for which there were no pictures. I knew so little. The rest I would have to imagine.

I began to clean up the mess of pictures. As I moved one old photo album, I was surprised to see on the table a copy of Giuseppe Conti's *The Pilgrim*. It was not the cheap paperback edition that I had read, but an unfamiliar hardcover with a black-and-white photograph of the author on the cover. When I opened the book a note fell out. "I thought this might comfort you in your time of grief." It was a gift to my mother from Sue Donovan, the helpful parishioner from Saint Cecilia's—no doubt a member of the Light herself.

Acting on impulse, I took the book and went outside. I walked the neighborhood for some time. It was close to midnight, and bedroom lights were flickering out in all the houses. I found myself on an overpass above the Grand Central Parkway as it approached the Triborough Bridge. I took out *The Pilgrim* and looked at the mesmerizing face of Giuseppe Conti. I watched the traffic speeding along on the highway beneath me.

As I stood there, the individual headlights of the passing cars became indistinguishable—a long, unbroken series of travelers racing in one direction, balanced by an identical, infinite line proceeding the opposite way. What was ahead of them or behind them that made them move so swiftly, so assuredly, sweeping across the provinces of the night? I imagined the stream of light passing beneath me and on into the dark landscape of New Jersey, and into the hills of Pennsylvania, and into the unseen heart of the country. And in the other direction, too, a stream of light moving up through Connecticut and Massachusetts, losing itself among the farthest reaches of the midnight coast, beyond Nova Scotia, beyond Newfoundland.

I turned to the middle pages of Giuseppe Conti's book and found a passage that had stuck in my mind. It now seemed strangely important:

I set my pack down on the ground and paused on the hill overlooking my family's mansion. I cringed to think of the horror that my life had become. I had lived in the thrall of death—obsessed by it, surrounded by it, terrified of it. Those who I thought loved me were my betrayers. I was trapped in a city of nightmares, a closed universe of lies and hidden meanings, where nothing was as it should be. How desperately I wanted to reject that life! But now I hesitated to depart. I thought of all that I would leave behind—my comfort, my ease, my absolute freedom. To reject all of this and debase myself on a search for truth would be ridiculous, the rash decision of a madman!

Thus did my thoughts run as I looked out over the city of my youth. But for all my hesitation, I knew I would never be satisfied if I abandoned my plan. I did not know enough about the world either to condemn it or to celebrate it. So I would embrace the unknown and lose myself in it. I would try to find, somewhere, a better way to live, a people who believe in peace, a truth that is conclusive. And if such things do not exist, then that too, in its difficult way, would be a discovery worth making.

I turned away from the world that I knew, ready now to begin. The road was dark, but the moonlight showed the way.

I closed the book and watched the highway, thinking that some tributary of that stream of light must also lead to Anna. To a decrepit motel in Nassau County, perhaps—or somewhere else by now; to a small room where a congregation is singing praise to God, or to a medical clinic in a forsaken land, or to a garden where a lovely voice is reciting the teachings of the Benefactor. Was she beyond finding? And somewhere else, even farther, past the last outposts of our explorations, my lost father.

I looked down at *The Pilgrim*, that impossible and exemplary book, and I felt a conviction arising within me, becoming clearer and clearer, almost against my will. What was freedom without Anna? What was the use of a life that would only bring awareness of everything I had lost? If I joined the Light they would probably let me see Anna within a few months, or maybe a year. Certainly I could give them that long.

I knew that when I found her she would again ask me to remain a member with her. I would simply have to make that decision when the time came.

Yes, I thought, I would return to the Imperium Luminis house and talk with Father Harrington about this and other things. He would fix me a cup of coffee and tell me a long story about Anna and me and my father and the Benefactor, and *his* version of the story would have a happy ending.

The lights on the highway were becoming blurry now, and closer to me. They seemed to surround me, to blanket me in their eternal glow. With a feeling of rapturous, long-sought surrender I imagined myself setting forth on a journey away from my life. I would leave that nightmare world behind me. I would become a pilgrim, so to speak. The lights were dancing all around me now, blinding me, leading me forward.

I was ready. Like the Benefactor setting off for an unknown territory, I was ready to begin. *Anna,* I thought, *I am coming to find you.*